I0460911

BEAUTIFUL RED

M. DARUSHA WEHM

Beautiful Red
by M. Darusha Wehm

published by *in potentia press*

Copyright 2007 M. Darusha Wehm

ISBN 978-0-9737467-1-6

http://darusha.ca/beautifulred

ONE

THE FIGURE STOOD beside Jack's bed and looked down at her sleeping form. Maybe she sensed his presence because she turned ever so slightly.

He leaned toward her, his 5 o'clock shadow nearly scratching against her chin. "Good morning, Jack," he said, his voice low and gravelly.

"What the fuck!" Jack woke up immediately, terrified and energized by the unexpected presence in her bedroom. She sprang toward the figure, jumping through his body and punching a button on the console sitting on the table at the side of her bed. The image of the intruder flickered once, twice, then disappeared.

Jack sat on the side of her bed, panting with exertion and adrenaline. "This alarm clock sucks," she said aloud, even though she was alone in the room. "That was no 'seductive stranger'," she said, reading the currently selected setting on the holographic Personal Wake-Me-Up unit by her bed. She punched a few buttons and selected 'chirping birds' from the scrolling menu of options charmingly titled "Who do you want to wake you up?".

"With my luck it's a fucking swarm of vultures." Jack hit save, blinked a few times and around her room.

The sun, such as it was, peeked through the window as the 'glass automatically turned from opaque to translucent. There hadn't been a decently bright day in years; it had been so long that Jack wondered if it were one of those nostalgic false memories that old people were notorious for sharing with anyone who would listen. "Back in my day," they would say, "the sky was blue and so was the ocean and everyone was happy and healthy and beautiful."

Bullshit, Jack thought. The air was always full of crap, even when she was a kid. Sure, it might have been bright, but it still stank and made people sick. At least no one got sick anymore. The vaccines took care of that.

Jack stood up and walked the ten paces to her tiny bathroom. She did what she needed to do then stripped off her underpants and turned on the shower. After washing the night's grime off both her body and the bathroom, she dried off under the blower and wandered over the eating area.

Calling it a kitchen would be an insult to the concept. She grabbed a breakfast bar out of the economy sized box near the fridge and slopped coffee into her cup. She pulled her uniform out of her autoclave and got dressed. Fucking blue daisy, she thought, distastefully, looking at the logo of her employer embossed on the back pocket of her regulation trousers. She wondered, not for the first time, if anyone at Bellis International had ever even seen a real daisy — blue, green or any other colour.

She stuffed half of the breakfast bar into her mouth and the other half into one of the utility pockets in her pants. On her way to the door, she went online by thinking the right combination of phrases to make it happen. The chips in her brain whirred and clicked; at least, Jack liked to imagine that they did something like that, but she couldn't actually feel or hear anything. She absentmindedly rubbed the area behind her left ear where the chips were implanted. She shuddered slightly as the image of her home workstation superimposed itself over her vision and her personal startup chime sounded in her ear.

She had a handful of messages from the night before, but she figured on reviewing them at her desk. Work had been dull at Bellis lately, so catching up on mail was a good way to ease into the day. Work at Bellis has always been dull, Jack thought, it just had been even more slow recently than it had been in the past. I guess there isn't a whole lot to secure these days, she thought, grabbing her jacket which was covered with the words Bellis International Security in large font, encircling an image of a sad looking blue daisy locked up in chains. Jack hated the blue daisy logo that Bellis slapped on everything, so she took a perverse pleasure in the Security department's version of the design.

Jack clomped down the stairs of her building, passing a couple of neighbours along the way. They did not acknowledge each other at all; Jack had never spoken to any of the other people who lived in her building. Most of the time everyone had that thousand yard stare that comes from paying 98 percent attention to their desktops and 2 percent attention to the physical world. Given proximity sensors and integrated global positioning and mapping systems, no one really had to pay attention to where they were going.

Jack pushed open the front door of the building, an old-school heavy door made of real glass and wood. There was no doubt that it was the nicest part of the building —— the interior was broken into tiny cubicle apartments, just like almost every other building in this city and every other city. Hardly anyone lived in more than 200 square feet of space per person and many people lived in less. But of all the shitty apartments she could have chosen, Jack liked this one. The building door was cool; you hardly ever saw real wood anymore and the amenities inside her tiny apartment were thoroughly up to date.

As she exited the building, Jack reflexively looked up and down her street. Her neighbourhood wasn't known to be particularly dangerous, but there were always people on the streets looking for handouts either by begging or by grabbing. Even though she rarely carried valuables, Jack wasn't about to be accosted. Partly it was common urban defensiveness and partly it was years of security training, as Jack scanned her lines of sight, checking for streeters while she moved purposefully down the street toward the train line.

Jack owned a second-hand electric scooter that she'd had an old friend of a friend modify to run hybridly on biodiesel for extra distance and speed, but parking was exorbitant everywhere and Bellis didn't spring for it for a lowly Security Officer Class 5. Only people high up in management, the kind who could afford parking on their own, got to have spots paid for by the firm. So Jack was waiting at the train stop, along with the rest of the downtown workers from her neighbourhood.

At least the trains were regular and fast. But their users paid the price of the trains' efficiency, which is that everyone used them, so they were usually crowded. As the next train whizzed to the stop, a small throng of people surged into its few small doorways and crammed into the already full cars. Jack found herself wedged between a young looking woman dressed in fashionable but inexpensive business wear and an older looking young man who was obviously a courier. He had skate shoes on and they looked well used but of excellent quality. Jack could hardly see the propulsion jets at the heels and couldn't see wheels at all. She recognized the man as one of the couriers that Bellis Corporate used.

His face and body fit her profile for attractiveness and if Jack had an entirely different temperament, she might have smiled at him. But while she was perfectly happy propositioning someone on the nets, she wasn't about to make an ass of herself on the train. Besides, he was clearly online, his gaze unfocussed but his face cloudy with a look of concentration.

The train ride downtown was mercifully short and Jack was expelled from the car along with a group of several other Bellis employees. She walked up to the main entrance to the office and heard the ubiquitous ping of her identity chip being recognized. This sound was immediately followed by another sound, this time of recognition that she was wearing a company approved uniform. Why they needed to have a chip on her ass when there was a perfectly good chip in her hand, she never would figure out.

She picked up a lift and got off on her floor. She walked down the corridor and opened the door to the Security Room. It sounded more interesting than most of the names on the firm's lobby directory, but it was really just another cube farm. She walked past a pair of identical cubicles until she reached the cube she shared with the night guy, Gilles. Bellis Security was a round the clock operation and each cubicle was shared by two staffers. They liked to keep a third of the cubes empty at any given time for cleaning staff and corporate monitors to visit them.

Jack suspected that the person who made up the cube assignments had a special sense of humour, putting her with Gilles. The falling down and breaking her crown jokes had just about finished and they had been sharing the desk for almost three years. She walked up to the desk and said, "Morning, G."

Gilles looked toward her, then adjusted his focus to look at her. "Morning, Jack," he replied, packing up his bag and gesturing for his coat. "It's been another dull one."

"Same old, same old," Jack replied, exchanging his jacket for hers on the coat hook. "It almost makes you long for the good old days, doesn't it?"

"You're too young to be nostalgic," he said, heading for the door. "The past only looks good when you can't see for shit. Later, dude." He shrugged on his jacket and loped down the hallway and out the door. Jack sat down in the chair and felt it automatically adjust to her preset configuration — a little lower, a little straighter and a whole lot softer. She settled in, taking out the second half of her breakfast bar and having a bite. The clock on the lower right corner of her display read 15:58 UTC.

• • •

Jack took a sip of her now cold coffee, made a face and put her cup down on the small ledge they called a desk. She unfocussed her eyes and logged into the Bellis system. Her vision was filled with an image which had essentially not changed since the technological bronze age — a rectangle with little pictures representing files and programs, a horizontal menu system and a yes and no interface. The desktop. Jack's nemesis.

Jack hated the desktop interface like some people hate liver. She had gotten into security the old-fashioned way — by subverting it for fun and profit. As a kid she liked to crack into other kids' systems, playing pranks and leaving messages. It was mostly harmless stuff, but she quickly realized that there were better ways to do almost everything. Once the Direct Connection became more common and monitors, mice and physical keyboards became obsolete, Jack expected a radical change in the way people interacted with their systems. But, no. They just emulated a WindowIconMousePointer system, drawing the desktop on the cornea rather than the screen. The lack of vision pissed her off.

She had configured her personal system to run with a home brew three dimensional interactive interface, but she was required to use the Bellis system at work. It caused her almost physical pain, but she turned on her "keyboard" by throwing a small switch on the side of her desk. A physical switch. She really hated that. A tiny laser light show started on her desk, showing the image of her custom keyboard

7

layout. At least they let her use her own keyboard layout. She tapped away, sensors on her desk picking up her movements and converting those motions to wireless input into her system.

She called up the mail system and paged through a bunch of garbage from the social committee and some messages from management about new business lines and appropriate branding imagery. Deleted. Jack opened up the systems viewer and watched the logs scroll by for a few minutes. She found the image calming and had been known to spot problems in their early stages just by having a feeling that the logs looked funny. They were looking fine today, so she opened up another window and started reading the news.

According to what she saw, there didn't appear to be a whole lot going on in the security world. Jack subscribed to all the usual trade feeds, the internal Bellis Security feed and she regularly visited a few outlaw cracker boards using an identity she first developed before she chose the right side of the law. Truth be told, she liked to keep her hand in on the lighter fun stuff and also figured that it didn't hurt to see what the other side was up to. Not that there really was an other side anymore.

Sure, code jockeys were still writing clever tools to break into systems and do a whole host of interesting things when they were in there. But ever since Everlock came on board, hardly any foreign bodies lived long enough to do any damage. It was like DDT for computer viruses. The end of an era

And it was both the best and worst thing that happened to the network security world. When Jack was a kid, security commanded respect and a decent salary to boot. Every firm was petrified that some cracker would break into their system and do stuff and they were willing to pay for the expertise to keep them out or get rid of them once they got in. But once Everlock was developed, network security became a lot less urgent.

Sure, every firm needed a security department and the staff still needed all those skills, but the willingness to pay for it vaporized like so much hot air. And markets being what they were, that meant that a security job went from being a high end career to a uniformed job. Really, security departments went from being filled almost exclusively with jobs for coders to being primarily concerned with law and order.

Since no one had yet come up with an Everlock for physical world crime, the bulk of security personnel were the equivalents of the anachronistic beat cops and squad detectives. Jack's group at Bellis was tiny in comparison to the field officers and they were treated according to their relative size. But Jack wasn't terribly bitter. The bottom had fallen out of network security before she was even out of school, so she went into the field with her eyes open. She just wanted to be able to stick her hands in the guts of the system and get paid for the privilege.

There hadn't been a lot of working with the guts lately, though, so Jack spent a lot of her time scanning the news and reading mail. She read about some firm trying a new system interface for its staff that used three dimensional motion for input. It sounded interesting and Jack was glad to see someone taking the risk, but the article made it sound like it wasn't going to last. A firm in Europe had several servers disappear, a self-professed good guy cracker in Africa was building tools to determine the provenance of the programs being eaten by Everlock and someone had built a fully functioning physical keyboard out of lego. It was a typical news day, but between reading the news while glazing at the logs, it ate up enough of the morning that Jack felt it was late enough to get another hotter coffee from the break room.

She stood, refocussed, and walked toward the tiny enclave which housed the coffee pot and a small fridge. She poured a cup and tried to ignore Tony, one of the other day staff. He was just a class 3 and he liked to talk about old fashioned fashion and nothing else. It was ultra boring stuff at the best of times and Jack was convinced he knew she hated it but talked her ear off anyway. She tried to get her coffee without arousing him, but it was not to be.

"You'll never guess what I just found on the boards," Tony gushed as he practically teleported next to Jack. He didn't wait for her to guess, but rather said, "A photo gallery of twentieth century Gucci shoes. All of them!" he practically squealed. Jack nearly threw he coffee at him, but said only "That's nice, Tony. Back to work," and walked back to her cube.

Tony was a character and Jack had to grudgingly admit that he added a little life to the office environment. His love of antiquated fashion went beyond websites and collectibles. He actually dressed as if he were from another era. His hairstyle and clothes looked like something out of an early first generation video show — short neat hair, white button up shirts, a flap of fabric hanging from his neck that he called a tie and eyeglasses. He even managed to find a way to make his regulation trousers seem old. Jack suspected he spent a lot of time at home with a fabric gun flattening pockets and tapering legs.

He wasn't completely antiquated, though. Like most people, he had several implanted diodes in his face, fashionably placed at his eyebrow, nose, lips, ears and cheeks. Really, he was an entertaining enough fellow, it was just that his obsession was a little bit too over the top for Jack, especially before her second coffee of the day.

Back at her desk, Jack started paging through Gilles' report from the night shift. Security officers were required to write up reports of their observations over the course of a shift and for the few times something did occur these reports were invaluable. Most of the time, though, the reports were either dull as the sky or read like the in-class messages of highschool students. Thankfully, the reports Gilles left fell soundly in the latter camp.

> 0800 UTC
> No anomalies to report. Still no water.
>
> 0830 UTC
> No anomalies to report. Henson in Pod 7 got a new haircut. Looks like a porcupine. Think I'm in love.
>
> 0900 UTC
> No anomalies to report. Looking forward to lunch.
>
> 0930 UTC
> No anomalies to report. Henson's hair ruined in the rain. It's over between us.
>
> 1000 UTC
> Eastern systems reporting fluctuations. They have a new sysadmin. Lucky to have access at all.
>
> 1030 UTC
> No anomalies to report.

And so on. Jack enjoyed Gilles' reports, particularly since they made up the majority of the conversation they ever had. Her own reports were generally less amusing but more well developed and

Jack felt that between their daily reports, she and Gilles had developed a friendship of a sort.

Later, she would check on the Eastern systems, mostly just to have something to do. The Eastern branch had their own Security department who was responsible for their systems, but since they interacted with the Western systems, a problem in one area could quickly become a problem in another area. But first she checked the video imaging logs for the night shift. She wanted to see Henson's new hair.

• • •

The Eastern system problems were exactly as Gilles had suspected — pebkac. Problem exists between keyboard and chair. The new admin misconfigured one of the databases to create multiple connections on each new action. It was a rookie mistake that looked a lot like a denial of service attack on the logs. Typical. Most of the actual problems Security dealt with were really just internal incompetence.

Jack spent the rest of the day reading Gilles' report and writing her responses, with a smattering of commentary on the logs and news of the day. There were no fires to fight today, just like it had been for a few weeks. There hadn't been any new hiring at the western branch of Bellis lately, so there hadn't been any noob errors to correct. It was comfortable, if boring.

Quitting time rolled around without any further interruptions from the other inmates; Tony had cornered Ravinder from Finance at one point, but Jack stayed out of their path. She packed her few personal items back into her pockets and after finishing off her report to Gilles, logged out of the Bellis system. The company's required daily run of Everlock quickly scanned her onboard system, a process which always slightly nauseated her. It was over soon enough, though and she marched out the door to the Security Room. Somewhere, on some log on someone else's field of vision, the note "TIMESTAMP 0102 UTC -- EMP 456873 -- EXIT" scrolled up and away.

TWO

AS JACK LEFT the building, the rain was falling lightly and making the streets shine in the dim late afternoon sun. Without even thinking, she opened up a program called "shades" from her home brew launcher and a dark platinum tinted screen rolled over her field of vision. To any bystander she looked like she had silver eyes — utilitarian but not very fashionable. The trendy look was to have glowing or animalistic prints on the outside of your shades, but Jack couldn't be bothered.

She started heading directly for the train stop, but was distracted by a sidewalk vendor selling spare electronics. The seller was obviously a scavenger, one of the many street people who eke out an existence on one or other side of the law, but always close to the line. The spare parts gleamed in the wet and Jack stopped to take a look. She wasn't working on any particular project, but you never knew when you might need something.

The seller had spread an old rug on the sidewalk and had arranged her wares carefully on top. Jack recognized this as a sign of someone who actually knew what she was dealing with, not just someone who will grab anything that looks like it may fetch a euro or two. Jack looked over the merchandise, waiting for something to catch her eye.

There was the usual array of those thin flexible screens that used to be used for portable monitors but now was really only used for clothes or wallpaper and a handful of nearly invisible add-ons that attached to implanted diodes. There were personal recorders, translators for several languages, taxonomic determinators and a whole host of devices Jack couldn't or chose not to identify by their overly large packaging. None of these interested her, although her hunch was right on the money — every item was good quality and up to date. She eventually picked up a small bag of what appeared to be small marbles.

"Are these what I think they are?" she asked the stall's minder quietly.

"That depends on what you think they are, doesn't it?" the streeter replied coyly. Jack grinned and asked if they were encrypted. "Of course," the vendor smiled, showing her crooked and rotten teeth. "What would be the point if they weren't?"

"Indeed," Jack said, "what would be the point? I'll take them." She pulled up her account, walking through a virtual gallery that appeared before her eyes. She stood before what looked like a statue of damned souls descending into hell. She saw her hands manipulating the statue, moving various parts of the figure in a complex pattern. The statue cracked open and its hollow space inside was filled with what appeared to be gold coins.

"How much," she asked, looking through the statue and coins to the scene on the other side, in the physical world. The vendor named a figure and Jack counted out coins. She saw herself handing them to a representation of the woman in her immediate focus, while the actual vendor shivered slightly as the upload took place, Jack's system wirelessly transferring the funds to the seller's account.

Jack still smiled to herself every time she paid for something. The statue and coins trick was a piece of user interface she had written herself along with the walking-through-the-museum representation. The whole gallery probably seemed more impressive than the funds transfer, but getting her home brew interface to hook up with the program that controlled personal accounts was more than a little difficult. The funds program was covered in layers and layers of security and average users weren't supposed to be able to play with it. They obviously didn't want people crediting themselves with extra funds, but they also weren't very keen on people modifying their user interfaces either.

Well, fuck 'em, Jack thought, as she slipped her bag of new micro video recorders into her pocket and headed back toward the train stop. She had no plan for the recorders, but had always wanted to try them out. They were tiny spheres that recorded and narrowcast audio and three dimensional video directly to their owner. Like almost everything else with a chip in it, they were connected to the everywherenet, the wireless network that connected everyone and everything everywhere. Using the nets, the recorders sent real-time images and sound to their owner using an encrypted signal. They had originally been developed for military espionage and police surveillance, but like everything else soon became available on the open market. Jack couldn't wait to try them out.

As she was waiting for the train, she noticed a couple of Security goons from another firm. It must be Lentech - only their cops wore that horrible crimson uniform. Jack thought they looked like packages of tomato flavoured soup as they grabbed some guy and patted him down. It was probably a private crime, since Lentech's offices were nowhere near the Bellis office and the guy looked more like a mugger or something rather than someone who made an enemy of a firm. He must have targeted a Lentech employee, so the firm's security cops went after him as a violator of The Law.

Jack thought she had read once that there was a book full of a bunch of different laws in a dusty cabinet somewhere, but the only law that was really enforced was the protection of employees from harassment. Like any other asset, employees needed to be protected from harm and part of any compensation package was the protection by the firms Security. This effectively allowed the Security departments of the various firms to arrest, detain and punish criminals. Some of the large cities still employed police departments, but they were really just Security for the city. Any offence against person or property was dealt with by the Security department of the victim's employer. They were tough on crime, so most people were perfectly happy with this arrangement.

The train arrived as the Lentech cops let the now beaten and bedraggled suspect go. Either he wasn't the guy or the offence was pretty minor. The train ride back to her neighbourhood was uneventful, though, and Jack spent most of the time online catching up on the underground cracker boards she followed. A couple of her online buddies were getting into a small conflagration over the Everlock tools being developed by the African cracker known as N$onow4. They were fighting about anything that could be argued — whether the tools worked, whether the job they purported to perform was useful, whether the Pope was Catholic. It was a typical day on the boards.

Jack scanned their arguments and moved on. She checked her mail and found a message from Adrian, a friend she had met on a board that specialized in talk about the role of intelligent agents in security, on both sides of the fence. They messaged each other most days and had real-time conversations a few times a week. Today's message read:

> "Hey J. Read about the missing crap in Brugges? Nets are full of it here, like some thieved h-ware is some great fucking scandal. Makes you wonder if there's more to it, right? Catch you tonight if you're free. A"

Jack always found Adrian's messages funny. She had no idea where "here" was, though a couple of years of context had narrowed it down to somewhere in Europe. Every time she asked, "Where are you," Adrian evaded the question. Jack wondered if the mystery was part of the charm; she suspected that it was. She knew that she would be disappointed if one day she found out that Adrian was the anonymous handle of, say, Tony the class 3. She shivered at the thought, then immediately dismissed it. Tony couldn't go two minutes without mentioning Chanel or Hilfiger, let alone two years.

Jack's onboard geophysical locator notified her that her train stop was coming up, so she logged out of her mail client by walking out of the Postal History section of the museum in which she saw herself. She refocussed on her surroundings and stepped to the door of the train. As it slowed into the stop, the door dissolved and Jack stepped onto the sidewalk. It was almost completely dark by now and she felt herself tense slightly with awareness of her surroundings. Things seemed pretty quiet on the street, but you could never be sure. She made it to the beautiful wooden door without incident, however, and it unlocked in response to the ping from her implants and a recognition of her biometrics.

She walked up the stairs to her floor, not bothering with the automatic firefighter's pole. She felt better getting some exercise, rather than letting the pole spiral her up to her floor. She approached her apartment door and heard the locks disengage in response to her proximity. Her apartment door wasn't wooden — that was just for the street door. The door to her unit was some kind of polycarbonite and it split down the middle disappearing into the walls on either side to let her in, then closed almost silently behind her.

Jack pulled the contents of her pockets out and dumped them on the side table by her bed. She took off the Bellis pants, shoved them in the autoclave and grabbed some more comfortable clothes out of her drawer. After she got changed, she opened up her fridge and grabbed a bottle of beer, opening it with a flick of her thumb. She drank a long swallow and threw a meal packet into the zapper. While the machine blinked and whirred, Jack picked up a fork with her physical hands and paged over to a site devoted to micro three-d video recorders with her virtual fingers. The zapper made its "done" noise and Jack pulled the hot food to her small table.

As she ate, she learned about how the recorders worked, not just how to deploy them and receive their output, but how to program them as well. By the time her food was gone, she was ready to start playing with her new toys. A chime sounded and she saw on her display that one of the paintings in her museum was blinking. She felt herself walk toward it and stand facing it. It took on the appearance of an old-school screen and text began to appear.

Incoming realtime secure message from ADRIAN:

>Hey J. You there?
>>I'm here, how's it going.
>Good, I guess. Things here are the usual. Everyone's all crazy about some such thing while roam burns. But that's the cost of life in the fast lane.

Jack smiled to herself. Subvocal recognition was so close to perfect that it was always amusing when it got things wrong.

>>Wish I were in the fast lane. Work is so boring I'm thinking of writing a bot to automate my breathing and then just put myself in some kind of hibernation.
>(laughter) Yeah, things haven't been the same since the bad guys actually got away with stuff. So what are you doing to occupy your mind?
>>Reading logs and reports, watching the boards, you know, the usual. You might be interested in this, though.
>Well? Spill it.
>>I picked up some micro recorders today from a streeter.
>Ooh, those are fun! Have you played with them yet?

>>No, I just got home when the usher started flashing.

The silent speech recognition software had problems with proper names. Jack had previously told Adrian about her home brew interface and explained that the message program was represented by an image of M. C. Escher's Sky and Water I, the famous line drawing of the fish and the birds. Ever since then, whenever they talked about getting messages, they referred to the Escher image.

>Well, then, I'll let you go so you can play with your new toy.
>>Sounds good. Maybe I'll flash the fish later.
>Once you get into the guts of those wee balls, you won't be doing anything else tonight. I'll flash you tomorrow.
>>OK. Later.
>Later.

The words scrolled up to the top of the frame, then the famous birds and fish slowly faded into view. Jack felt herself turn and walk toward the museum's door. As she passed through the door, the image of the museum faded and she became more aware of her real surroundings. She was sitting in her chair with a third of a beer and a dirty plate in front of her. She blinked, had a swallow of beer and reached for the sack of marbles.

Jack picked up one of the units and rolled it between two of her fingers. It was pale blue, lighter than the colour of the Bellis logo and it shimmered with an iridescence when the light glanced off it. It was small and round, about the size of a marble, but covered in hundreds of tiny spheres. Each one of the little nubs was a self-contained camera, capable of recording three dimensional video and audio. Taken together, the unit could wirelessly narrowcast up to a thousand still images at once or create an immersive three dimensional recording in real time.

Jack looked closer and adjusted the magnification of her vision to 10 times normal. She inspected the tiny ball, looking for markings, imperfections and seams — anything, really that made it look different from a pale blue raspberry. She found the tiny depression you could use to open the unit and also caught a glimpse of what appeared to be a logo. She adjusted her vision to a greater magnification and saw that the logo looked like a stylized B created in lace.

She didn't recognize the brand, but she had been out of the hardware market for a while so she was not surprised. She slipped a thin tool into the opening crevice and gently pried open the sphere. The recorder split in half, revealing tiny circuits and what were almost certainly clusters of nanotubes. Jack noticed a slight gleam on one side and increased her magnification even more.

"There you are," she said aloud, having found the uplink code. She copied and pasted it to her scratch pad and closed up the sphere. She sat back and was momentarily disoriented as she refocussed her eyes back to normal magnification. The brief sense of vertigo passed and she took another swig of her beer. She called up an underground board devoted to micro recorders and ran a search for the latest version of a well known controller program. She quickly scanned the file with her own copy of Everlock as well as her homemade scanner that searched for less malicious but equally annoying bits of unexpected code, then when it was pronounced clean, she downloaded the software to her own system.

As it started up, she was immediately impressed by the interface. No kludgy windows and menus here. Rather, it was a graphical representation of a recorder — a nice, shiny sphere with an obvious entrance slot. She navigated to the slot and felt herself drop into the sphere. Once inside, she was in a maze that clearly mimicked the circuits in the real recorders. The maze was well marked, however and at the first door she encountered a reassuring voice pleasantly offering a tutorial.

Jack usually eschewed wizards and walkthroughs, but this program was unlike anything she had used before. And more importantly, the programmer in her was dying to find out what the tutorial would look like. She audibly said the word "yes" and immediately the door opened revealing what appeared to be a nice looking young man.

"Hello," he said, "I am the tutorial." He offered his hand and Jack shook it. The warmth and firmness of his grip surprised and delighted Jack. This is great work, she thought. "Are you a new user, or would you like to go straight to the advanced features?" he asked.

Let's see what he can do, Jack thought to herself. "I've never used a micro recorder before," Jack said, " but I'm a Security Officer Class 5 and I've done some complex UI programming. I don't think I need the dumbed down tour."

The tutorial was frozen for a microsecond, then said, "I am sorry. I did not understand your last sentence. However, as a new user, you may find the complete tour most beneficial. Please, follow me." He started walking down the corridor and Jack thought to herself that the designer was clearly better at mimicking tactile sensation than verbal interface. Oh well, she thought, I can waste a few minutes on the full meal deal.

The new user's tour took only about twenty minutes and Jack had to admit that she probably would have an easier time working with the recorders after having gone through the process. In fact, by the time she felt herself leave the sphere, the micro recorder in front of her on the table was fully configured to use.

She went to get a water and a snack and quickly checked the recorder. For a disconcerting moment, she was watching herself perform the very actions she was currently doing — getting a slice of toast from the food machine and pouring water into a tumbler. There was absolutely no noticeable lag. It was amazing technology, that she could not deny.

It made her wonder, as she turned off the program, what kind of surveillance devices were in use in the wild. Surely, if marble-sized recorders could be bought on the street corner, organizations with money and clout could afford to buy or create even smaller ones, maybe even the size of a speck of dust. A person could be constantly watched and recorded and never know.

She dismissed the thought as soon as it was fully formed, though, because the point was moot. Round-the-clock ever-present surveillance had become the norm years ago. As soon as everywherenet became truly ubiquitous, any illusion of privacy that people harboured was finally dissolved for good. Your body's actions may not be photographed as such, but your location, any programs you are running, any conversations you are having are logged and trackable. Even, to a certain extent, your thoughts.

Sure, no one had the time or energy to truly monitor most people, but you could never really be alone. And for law enforcement or in case of emergency, the logs could be reviewed. They were destroyed after a week as a matter of course, but would be retained longer for important people or known criminals. It was the cost (or benefit, depending on your perspective) of having an always accessible and free to use network.

Beautiful Red

Jack pushed these thoughts out of her mind and thought instead about bed. It was Tuesday, which meant that tomorrow was her last workday for the week. She was looking forward to the three days off; there was no doubt that ten days of working in a row was unpleasant, even if the hours were reasonable. Some of her colleagues at smaller firms or lower classes worked ten or more hours a day. As much as she hated Bellis, she recognized that it could be a whole lot worse somewhere else.

She stripped off her clothes and stuffed them in the autoclave. It was on a timer and would flash clean everything inside while she was sleeping. She double checked the alarm and again doubted the wisdom of the holographic Personal Wake-Me-Up. Still, there's nothing like an adrenaline rush first thing in the AM. Damn that subconscious, she thought and took a gulp of SleepingJuice. She knew she only had about five minutes until it kicked in, so got into bed and ordered the windows to darken and the lights to dim. The next thing she knew, she was asleep.

OOOOI

I'M STARTING TO get scared. I'm getting worried for my sanity. Maybe I'm paranoid and there's a hundred boards all devoted to this, this — what would you even call it, a syndrome? Can't even run the search, though, too scared about what I might find. What if I'm the only one, or even worse what if this is the beginning of some incurable illness, brain cancer or some chemical thing. Christ, I think I'm losing it. You know, nuts, batty, loony, crazy, wacko. That's what I think I am. Crazy.

It's been happening for a few weeks now, on and off. Everything seems normal, everything is fine, then wham! It's like nothing I've ever experienced before. Literally.

It's later. Everything is fine and then bam, it's some random amount of time later. And I have absolutely no idea what I've been doing and no sense at all that any time has passed.

At first I just ignored it. Maybe I was really bored and the time just escaped on me. That can happen, right? But after it happened a few times I couldn't ignore it anymore. If I'm at the office when it happens I'll casually ask someone about the last hour or two; you know, make it sound like I was zoned out and wasn't paying attention. They'll say that everything was normal; I guess I didn't run around like a monkey or start foaming at the mouth or anything. But I just don't remember it. At all.

I'm thinking about looking at my logs, but you can't just call them up like you're paging over to some board. You have to ask for them, officially. I don't know if I have the skills to get them undetected. Oh, I could get them, but I can't be sure I wouldn't leave a trail. And I can't be found out. I need to not be crazy.

Beautiful Red

I've seen those people. The streeters. The ones who clearly were normal once then they lost it and now they're nowhere. Living like rats. Well, I won't be a rat. I'd die first. Die.

THREE

THE BIRDS WEREN'T that bad after all. They really did just chirp and about three of them flapped benignly over Jack's bed until she hit the off button on the alarm. "I can live with that," she said, getting out of bed and padding to the bathroom.

She went through the usual morning paces and was out the door within fifteen minutes. She washed down half her breakfast bar with coffee as she headed for the train stop. The morning was pretty much the same as every other day, maybe a few more streeters than before. It seemed like there were more streeters every day. It was hard to tell if it just seemed that way; if there were any official stats on the number of street people, they were classified and unreported. Most people were thankful for what they had and didn't like to think about the alternative.

When Jack got into the office, Gilles was finishing up the night shift report. "Anything good for me?" Jack asked.

"Eastern systems are fubar again," Gilles said, getting his jacket on. "Nothing for us though. We've got the Eastern noobs locked out for now."

"Noobs," Jack said, derisively. "You'd think that by now they'd give a half a day orientation at least. It would cost a fraction of what it costs to clean up the mess."

"That's corporate, for ya," Gilles said, "don't know their ass from Tuesday. Later, dude." He left the Security Room and Jack settled into the chair. When she first started at Bellis, she was put off by the cubicle sharing system. Fresh out of training, she idealistically believed that companies would have realized that physical presence in the office was obsolete thinking. But now that she had been working in the system for a while, she realized that it wasn't solely a lack of understanding that made corporate require physical presence.

It was a method of control. Sure, the network was able to ensure you actually were working when you were on the clock; no one had to physically see you to be sure of that. But making you wear the uniform, sit in the chair and just be there is a not so subtle way of letting you know who's in control. You really gave up a lot of freedom in exchange for employment and all the historical trappings just helped to break your spirit a little more.

But really, what other option did you have? Become a streeter? No-one chose that life, never mind what those conservative vidcasters said. Jack daydreamed about other options all the time, which is to say that she daydreamed about nothing. She wished things were different, but wishes don't make anything real, so she tried to find satisfaction where she could. Work wasn't doing it for her these days, but between the boards and online friends she had an okay social life. Maybe playing with the micro recorders would keep her occupied for a while — learning a new tool usually interested her for a few weeks or months. She might have to visit that street vendor more often.

Jack spent the work day paging through the boards, reading Gilles' report and avoiding Tony. The first two items were more successful than the latter, as he accosted her not once but twice on the way to the washroom with boring anecdotes about some guy in Cuba with a collection of what she had to assume were clothes, though she'd never heard the word he used before. At least he was benign. Unlike that guy in admin, Atomu, who was obsessed with practical jokes. Having an anti-grav chip stuck to the bottom of your chair was one thing, but he had graduated to doing things like screwing with the access codes and turning entire logs into haiku.

Jack hadn't seen any of his shenanigans first hand and she was thankful. She wasn't sure if he just hadn't made his way up to her floor, or if he was scared of Security. Privately, she found his handiwork pretty funny; she just knew that it would make her life momentarily miserable if it happened on her watch.

Around mid-afternoon, as she was fighting off the end of the day drowsiness, Jack noticed something odd. The Eastern systems were still being flaky, which meant that the problem had been going on for over 36 hours. That was a long time, even for a really green noob. Jack punched up the logs for the Eastern system, entering her Class 5 admin token. She knew that action would be flagged for her counterpart in Eastern and she expected an angry message any minute now, complaining about her interference. She just couldn't let it go by unchecked — it was the closest thing to something actually interesting that had happened in ages.

As she suspected, her messenger started chirping a few seconds after she accessed the logs. She ignored the insistent sound resonating insider her eardrums and started reading.

That's strange, she thought, looking at the logs. There's no record of anything wrong here. The logs look like any others. Hell, they look just like mine. The insistent sound of the messenger brought her back to reality and she finally answered.

"Hey, Jack," the voice at the other end said, sounding surprisingly calm.

"Sorry, Mac," Jack said, "I just couldn't stay out of it. I know it's none of my..."

Macintyre, the Eastern Class 5, cut her off. "I'm not calling to bust yer balls," he said, "I'm hoping you've got a clue what the fuck this is all about."

"Damn, I don't know," Jack answered. "This log looks fine. Are you sure the system's borked?"

"Only completely," Mac answered, the frustration clear in his voice. "Users can only log in half the time, then they get kicked off. But no one seems to be able to replicate the problem. It's totally random. Yesterday's crap didn't help, but this doesn't seem to be related to that. I don't know what this is."

"I haven't seen anything like this in years," Jack said. "I know it's an old school idea, but have you thought about shutting it down and restarting the system?"

Jack heard a sharp intake of breath from the Eastern guy. "Christ, that's drastic." He paused. "But I'm running out of options. I'll see if we can't straighten it out some other way, but if it come to that, I'll let you know."

"Thanks, Mac," Jack said. "I'll keep an eye on things from my end, if you don't mind."

"I'll take all the help I can get," he said and ended the message. Jack sat back and watched the clean-looking Eastern logs scroll.

• • •

Mac never did figure it out, but by the time the middle shift was arriving, the Eastern systems had gone back to normal. Jack had spent the remainder of the afternoon scrutinizing the logs from her systems and for the Eastern systems and finally noticed something odd — a connection on the Eastern side from an external node. Of course, access to the system was restricted to authenticated users, but if you could authenticate to the system you could log in from anywhere. You wouldn't get credit for being at work of course, but you could always work if you wanted to. Obviously, not many people took advantage of this feature, so it was unusual enough that Jack instinctively noticed, even though the system wouldn't flag this kind of connection.

On a hunch, Jack ran the address through a secure reverse lookup feature she had installed in a fairly well-hidden directory. Bingo. The address resolved to Buyside Solutions Inc., a huge financial services corporation with branches in every major centre. As far as Jack could figure, there was no good reason why someone would access the Bellis system from within the Buyside system, unless someone from Buyside was trying to get access to private Bellis documents.

Jack paged over to her office mail and rooted through her deleted messages looking for the most recent "What's New at Bellis Corporate" propaganda piece. She scanned the last few weekly missives and read between the lines. It looked like it was possible that Bellis was planning on acquiring a new subsidiary. Jack wasn't involved in big finances, no one who wore a uniform could afford to be, but she knew enough to realize that inside poop would be pure platinum to an outfit like Buyside.

Espionage. What a cute, antiquated concept. But, if she could foil an attempted acquisition of unauthorized information, she would get bumped up to Class 7 or 8 without breaking a sweat. But she had to tread carefully, since she could never survive a lawsuit from Buyside. And that was if they didn't just sic their goons on her instead.

Jack left coded notes about the situation for Gilles in her report and made a note for herself to message him privately the next day. She logged off the network, got her jacket and headed out the door.

She didn't have a fully formed plan about how to investigate this, but she hadn't felt this engaged in her work in years. Maybe ever.

On her way home she stopped off at a take away that made food the old fashioned way, with multiple ingredients grown from seed rather than flavoured nutrient blocks. She spent half a day's pay on a small box of steaming vegetables, part of her weekly indulgence. She carefully carried the box back to her apartment, keeping a keen eye on the streeters aroused by the aroma. She made it into her apartment unmolested and shucked her uniform immediately.

Changed into her own clothes, she popped a beer from the fridge, set her display to rest and sat at the table with her stir-fry. She ate slowly, savouring the flavours. She knew that some people ate like this every day and that knowledge more than anything else made her angry about the inequities in the world. But many people could never afford to eat this food even once and Jack was aware of the realities of life enough to know this as well. Once she had finished every last morsel and had her last sip of beer, she stuffed the box and bottle into the recyclatron. She did nothing for a moment, enjoying the memory of her dinner, then restarted her display.

She started up the program that controlled the micro recorders and spent the next three hours breaking it. Part way through her fourth hour of trying, she finally successfully reconfigured it the way she wanted and involuntarily let out a small yelp of happiness over her success. She wanted to share her victory as well as talk about what she had uncovered at work, so she pinged Adrian.

"Not available", came the response, "do you want to leave a message?" Jack said, "No" and went to one of the micro recorder boards instead. She paged through a few posts, but the board was publicly accessible, if hard to find and presumably logged, so she left without posting anything.

She silently cursed herself for being her usual antisocial self and never asking Gilles for his private contact information. Logically she knew that no one ever did that at work; off duty fraternization was frowned upon strongly enough that no one ever bothered. But now the social code of work had become inconvenient. She would have to contact Gilles tomorrow at the office.

She sat in her apartment, the night sky barely visible even though her window was still transparent and cracked another beer. After drinking half of it, she opened her fridge and its freezer compartment. She found a small box labeled "petite green peas" and opened it. Inside she fished out a cigarette from her small stash.

Tobacco was illegal, of course, although no one ever got in trouble for simple possession anymore because possession didn't pose a problem to any of the firms. Even so, a record of criminal activity can be a real problem for someone in Security, so Jack was slightly paranoid about her stash.

She lit the contraband cigarette and spent the next ten minutes thoroughly enjoying her illicit habit. She didn't even smoke once a week, but sometimes it played a part in her weekend indulgences as an extra treat. The drug was an acceptable substitute for companionship and it almost compensated for not being able to talk about her exploits; however, between the nicotine and the alcohol, she felt like she had taken half a hit of SleepingJuice. She fell into her bed, excited and intoxicated and oddly a little sad. She set the alarm for the middle of the night, then immediately fell asleep and dreamed of infinitely scrolling log files.

FOUR

JACK WOKE AGAIN to the chirping birds, each peep sounding a bit like a tiny jackhammer to her aching head. The first morning of the weekend often started this way, though usually a few hours later. She silenced the birds, rubbed her eyes and banged her way through her tiny apartment to the water. She drank down a couple of glasses and tried to convince herself that she felt better. She grabbed a hot breakfast packet from the box and chucked it in the zapper. She turned on the coffee and while everything was heating up, she found some comfortable clothes. The zapper dinged and the coffee machine pinged and Jack took her food and drink to the table. She ate and drank offline, becoming less aware of her headache, more aware of her surroundings and thinking subconsciously about the previous day's revelations.

She knew what was going to do, she just didn't want to admit it to herself. Security was a good job, that was sure, and promotion would make it an even better job. Hell, she might even be able to move to an apartment with a bedroom. Or eat real food more than once a week. But none of that was worth committing a crime. Jack was fully aware of that, but she also knew that the real motivation for what she was going to do had nothing to do with Bellis, her job or any of the other possible gains. The real reason was that it was exciting. It was what she had trained for and it was what she had done for fun before she got into security. It made her brains throb and her skin itch, but in a good way.

She was going to break in to Buyside. It was either break in or forget the whole thing. Technically there was no crime in just connecting to the Bellis system since all users had to authenticate and the actual connection was out of her jurisdiction, anyway. But she knew something was up and she had to find out what it was. She had to get in there and she had to get out again without being caught. This was going to be fun.

She fired up her display and headed straight for the Escher. She set the basic encryption on and tunnelled into the Bellis system through the security back door. She messaged Gilles as soon as she was in. He answered immediately.

>Hey, dude. Read your report. Not surprised you called.
>>You saw it, too?
>Yup. Weird. Nothing wrong with it, though, officially.
>>Dunno...
>Me neither. You going in?
>>
>
>>How did you know?
>Don't read someone's reports every day and not figure out a thing or two.
>>Back me up?
>'Course.

Jack let out the breath she didn't realized she'd been holding. She wasn't so sure you could know a person from daily reports and shift change banter. He could have just as easily laughed her off as offered to help. She drank a little water and forced her heart to slow down.

>>I'll set up a secure voice line between us. What's your handle?
>aces04
>>aces04?
>I play cards.
>>OK whatever. You'll know me as jackalantrn.
>Cool. Later, dude.

Jack disconnected and on her display saw herself walk over to the main entrance to the museum. There was a wall of archaic telephones with seats in front of them. She sat at one and lifted the receiver. "jackalantrn to aces04, secure," she said into the mouthpiece and almost immediately heard Gilles' voice as if he were in the room with her.

"Hey, J," he said, "what's your plan?"

"I'm going to break in to Buyside's system and find out who or what was connecting to our Eastern system," she said matter of factly.

"Okay," he answered, "I figured that. But I was wondering more specifically how you were going to accomplish that."

"Leave the details to me," Jack said, "but I'll need you to monitor the nets to see if I'm leaving any traces and let me know what their security are up to."

"Can do," Gilles said, "keep me posted and let me know if there's anything else I can do. We can't be letting them catch you, now. I don't want to have to put in the overtime."

Jack laughed and started heading toward Buyside's system. Her three dimensional interface was theoretically good enough to render anything on the nets, but she had never tried anything as complex as a major corporate system. Her program automatically looked up architectural plans for Buyside's buildings and rendered them as the embodiment of the system. It would never be a perfect representation — extra rooms would have to be created or corridors filled in, but it beat WIMP or even a command line by a country mile.

The rendering engine was pretty fast and as Jack felt herself walking toward the horizon, she saw the building grow in front of her. There were guards patrolling the perimeter, representations of the firewall that protected the system. "There should be a break around the 357th node," Gilles said.

"How do you know?" Jack asked, staying out of the guards' field of vision.

"You're not the only one with mad skills, you know," he said, chuckling. "Most of us security old timers got our start hacking." Jack had forgotten that Gilles was significantly older than she was, a fact easy to forget in this era of wrinkle resistant skin and de rigeur body modification.

"Sorry, man," she said, "I'll head for the three five seven." She snuck around the side of the building and was beginning to wonder if Gilles was as competent as he claimed to be when she saw it. A tiny area unpatrolled by guards, where if she approached it just right, they wouldn't be able to see her for the shrubbery and shadows. She crawled over to the break and when she got to the building she found a small grating in the side of the wall.

"Crap," she said, "I need tools. I'll have to go back. Hang on."

"No, don't," Gilles said, "what do you need?" Jack rattled off a list of well known cracker scripts and a few utilities that just happened to be very useful. In a couple of seconds, Jack felt the unmistakable heaviness of a download. "That should do," Gilles said, "I just dumped my toolbox on you."

Jack looked down and saw a small brown sack materialize at her feet. She opened it and smiled at the contents — programs rendered as physical tools. The sack included a few lengths of pipe, some bits of wire, boltcutters, putty, dog biscuits, wire cutters, one of those reinforced paper biohazard suits, a couple of knives and even a handgun. Jack wondered what types of shenanigans Gilles got up to with this toolbox.

She pulled out the wire cutters and got to work on the grate. The blades were sharp and well oiled and she was through in a few seconds. She stuffed the cutters back in the bag which she strapped to her belt. "I'm in," she said as she crawled into the duct, pulling the remains of the grate behind her to cover her tracks.

"All quiet on the Eastern front," Gilles said, softly. Jack grunted her understanding and continued crawling into the building. She was using dual imaging, a technique that most people had become accustomed to and people in her line of work found to be like a second nature. Technically, one image was projected on one eye while simultaneously a second completely different image was projected on the other. After some practice, a person could get pretty good at watching two different things at the same time, with almost one hundred percent attention on both. Jack was seeing the graphical representation of herself cracking Buyside's system while simultaneously paging through a spec document she'd unearthed some time ago detailing the creation of a standard corporate system.

She knew that this system would be slightly different and could theoretically even have been designed from scratch, but she was banking on the general lack of innovation in the corporate world preventing any radical modifications on the usual design. If she were lucky and the original Buyside designers were typical, there should be a grating to her left in about a metre, which should open into a cache that was on the other side of the authentication barrier.

It looked like the Buyside designers were true to form as she reached the grating. She whispered, "Here goes nothing," and clipped away with the wire cutters. The grating fell to a clang a story below her. Jack held her breath, then whispered to Gilles, "Anything on the radar?"

"Nope," he said, "it's like there's nothing there."

"Good," she said. "I think I'll be okay." She dropped into the cache and found herself in a cavernous warehouse space, filled with books in shelves, filing cabinets stuffed with documents, old monitors hanging on the walls showing scrolling logs and boxes and boxes of who knows what. Small boxes and documents continually fell out of a small hole in the ceiling into a pile that was sorted and filed by small drones. They paid no attention to Jack.

She found the door and listened for footsteps from the other side. She knew that the imaging construct didn't represent activity audibly unless there were also visuals, but natural habits are hard to break. She put on the light gloves from Gilles' toolbox and pushed the door open. The hallway was empty and she stepped into it, almost expecting klaxons to go off and emergency lights to illuminate the hall with pointers to her location. But the door merely swished shut behind her and the hallway remained dark.

According to her spec document, the hallway she was in was an admin area that branched into the area of the system from which the strange login had originated. It was a low security area, which was helpful for Jack, but was curious. Jack followed the spec as if it were a map, turning right and left according to its directions.

Things were going smoothly, maybe a little too smoothly, she thought. All of a sudden she saw something approach her from around the next corner. It wasn't a person, which made sense. There would be no reason for an admin to the poking around in here. It looked sort of like an android and sort of like a drone. It was about half Jack's height and one and half times her width, with arms and legs like a humanoid machine but it nowhere near as elegant as an android. But more importantly, it was followed by several others just like it.

"Gilles," she whispered urgently.

"Yeah, I see it," he answered, "don't worry. It's just the cron jobs running. They won't notice you."

Jack knew intellectually that this was true, but she still held her breath as the first robot went past her. It didn't even slow down, but made a bee line for one of the corridors. Its compatriots followed suit, heading in their own preprogrammed directions. When the last one had passed, Jack let out her breath and continued following her route. After a few minutes more of twists and turns, she found herself at a door which read Client Service Delivery System. "That's odd," Jack said.

"What?" asked Gilles.

"It looks like the login came from the Client Service Delivery System," she answered, "that sounds like it should be an input only area."

"Hmm..." Gilles said, "I'll see if I can track anything down about it. I'll get back to you." Jack double checked her spec and her notes on the logs from the Bellis Eastern system. This was the place all right. Jack walked up to the door, drew her breath and pushed it open.

On the other side was a circular room with what looked like racks and racks of disk. There was clearly a lot of data being stored here, but the buckets of data were hardly the most interesting part of the room. It was all the doors. There were doors all the way around the wall, door after door after door. As Jack thought about it, it made sense. Client systems usually had to accommodate a large number of connections simultaneously, so this room needed a lot of entrances to let the clients in.

Fair enough, she thought and started to look around. At first everything seemed normal, but then she noticed a few things out of place, items that shouldn't be there. There were a few items on the floor that looked suspiciously like the tools she herself was carrying. There was a part of what may have been a glass cutter over by one of the racks. Jack picked it up carefully, wrapped it in a tissue and slipped it into her bag. Looking further, she found a rectangle of wood, which she popped into her bag as well. She thought she had found everything when she spotted what appeared to be a piece of paper stuck under one of the doors on the other side of the room. She pulled it out and saw that it was a map, similar to the spec document that she herself was using.

The partial map gave Jack an idea. "Gilles," she said.

"I'm here," came the reply.

"Can you get a hold of an accurate spec of the BS CDS?"

"Should be able to," he answered, "those things are usually semi-public. Just sit tight and I'll get it for you." Jack looked around the room. Who are you, she wondered. How did you get here and what did you want? "Got it," Gilles said, "it should be coming down now."

Jack's head felt a little heavier then became normal again. She called up Gilles' download and pulled a blueprint of the room she was in out of her bag. Unlike the spec she had been using, which showed this area as simply a room, Gilles' map was accurate down to the number of disks on each rack.

Jack held the map up before her eyes, then removed it from her field of vision and compared the two images. Identical. She turned around slowly, comparing what she saw. Same, same, same, different, same... wait. Something was different, but what was it? The doors. The doors were wrong somehow, but how. There were doors all the way around the room and it was the same in the map.

Jack looked down then up, then it dawned on her. Too many doors. There were too many doors in the room. She counted the doors and the map, then counted the doors in the room and that confirmed it. There was an extra door in here. She compared the map and the room again, this time specifically looking at the doors and she found it. The extra door. "Gilles," she said.

"I'm here," he answered, "what's up?"

"Things might get weird in a second."

"What are you doing?" he asked, sounding concerned. Jack didn't answer, but just opened the extra door. She stepped across the threshold and the moment when she knew there was nothing beneath her feet and that she was going to fall seemed to last forever. There was nothing on the other side.

"Oh, shit."

FIVE

WELL, THAT WAS fucking unnerving," Jack said, sitting at her table in her apartment, nursing a growing headache and a slight case of nausea.

"What happened," Gilles asked, "are you okay?"

"I'm fine," Jack replied, having a sip of water, "I just felt what it was like to be, I don't know, deleted, I guess. Weird. Did anything show up at your end?"

"Not really," he said, "I caught a strange blip on the log but it didn't get flagged or anything so you're probably okay."

"Cool," Jack said, rolling her neck and working out the kinks of being essentially away from her body for a couple of hours.

"Did you find anything," Gilles asked.

"Yeah," Jack said, "there were some artifacts left behind from what look like cracking tools and then there's the extra door."

"Door?" Gilles asked, "What do you mean, door?" Jack hadn't told him about her representational interface system and now didn't seem to be the time to explain it.

"Node, I mean," she said, "there were too many connection nodes. Well, just the one too many. I tried to access the extra one and got booted off the system. That's how I ended up back here."

"That explains what I saw," Gilles said. "So what's the plan now?"

"I'm going to sift through the stuff I found and see what comes up," Jack said, "You don't have to stay on with me; go home or whatever."

There was a slight pause. "I am home," Gilles said, "the shift ended almost an hour ago."

"Oh, crap, I'm sorry," Jack said, "I didn't mean to pull you into this on your own time."

"It's okay," Gilles said, "it was fun. Let me know if you need any help with the stuff you found. Otherwise, I'll catch you next week."

"Thanks, Gilles," Jack said, "I should be okay. Have a good week-end."

"You, too," he answered, "Later, dude." He disconnected and Jack went offline. She was sweating and her mouth tasted like something died in it. She drank some water and stripped off her soaked clothes, stuffing them in the autoclave. She went into the bathroom, closed the door and turned the shower on. She stood under the misting water for longer than the suggested maximum, making a mental note to skip a shower tomorrow so she wouldn't reach her water quota before the end of the month.

When she finally felt refreshed, she dried off and stepped back into her room. She threw on some fresh clothes and got a piece of toast. She sat at her table, still offline, and thought. There were crackers in that system and they were almost surely the ones connecting to the Bellis system. But why?

She opened up the logs from the Bellis system and looked at the outgoing connections. There it was — a connection to another system, this one somewhere in Benelux. Jack couldn't get a fix on what system it was exactly; it didn't look corporate, which was even stranger. But it certainly indicated that Bellis wasn't the final target.

She finished her toast, drank some more water and got another carafe of coffee going. When it was ready, she poured a cup and re-connected. She opened up Gilles' tool bag and picked out the items she had found on the scene in Buyside's Client Delivery System. She looked at the scrap of map and recognized it as a part of the same spec that Gilles had found for her. She made a note to ask him where he got it. She carefully put it aside and pulled out the other items.

Now, these were more interesting. There was a two by four beam, an odd representation, really, but Jack got it in one — jam it in the door and it's a tool to keep the connection open. She ran it through her command line editor and confirmed that it was a script to stop a connection from closing. She then turned her attention to the fragment of a blade.

She guessed it was a kind of glass cutter, but that was mainly from context. She had seen something similar in a first aid kit once, used to cut off clothes, presumably. She ran it through the command line and opened it up. It was a fragment of code and reading it through she could guess that it was a kind of high-end break and enter tool. She searched the nets for the snippet, but got back no results. Not surprising, since it was obviously a serious cracker's piece of code, maybe even written just for this job.

But why break into a Client Delivery System, when the content in there is available for a fee in a second and for free with a little digging on the nets? And why log in to the Bellis system once inside? As she was pondering this, Jack was distracted by the Escher print's flashing. She answered, expecting Gilles and instead saw:

> Incoming realtime secure message from ADRIAN
>
> >Hey, J.
> >>A., hi, how's it going?
> >Not bad. How are the micros?

Jack had completely forgotten about her new toys in the last day's excitement. She started to talk about her recent activities, but at the last minute stopped herself.

> >>Man, I had a bitch of a day yesterday. I've just been too wiped out to do anything really, past poking around in the program - I haven't even taken them out of my apartment yet.
> >Damn, I'm disappointed. I was hoping for some juicy amateur porn from the break room.
> >>Eww. Don't even say that. The horrible images. I'm not going to be able to use that place for a week now.
> >(laughter) Well, just don't forget to fill in your old buddy when you do test drive those things, okay.
> >>No problem, pal. You'll be the first.
> >Cool. Later.
> >>Later.

Jack disconnected. She felt a little guilty about keeping her excitement from Adrian, but she knew that she may have just stumbled upon something no one had seen for years, not since the days before the everywherenet. Someone had used the BS CDS as a screen, a diversion. They had logged in to the Buyside system as a way of covering their tracks. Jack figured that the connection to the Bellis system was the same thing — the crackers were just making a long trail of logins to make it harder to trace back to their real origin. It was weird, buy until she knew more she wanted to keep it all for herself.

Jack was certain she had heard of this before somewhere, so quickly searched the nets. Sure enough, back in the days before the everywherenet, when IP addresses were assigned to machines not places, you had this kind of thing all the time. But now that the wireless net was, well, everywhere, you didn't need to hide your tracks. All you had to do was physically move. Though, of course, your own personal log would show where you had been, both physically and on the nets, so the point was really moot.

So, if you couldn't ever really hide, what would be the point of this exercise? Jack rubbed her face, got up and tried to pace across her tiny floor. Every time she figured something out, a new problem would crop up. It was maddening. And more interesting than anything she had done in years.

She needed to take a break, though. She was just going around and around in circles coming up with more questions than answers, so she had to stop. She called up her news aggregator and started idly paging through the various things around the world that people had flagged as interesting.

Most of it was not actually all that interesting, but that was typical. The trouble with relying on the combined wisdom of other individuals was that no one had the exact same interests as you, so either you limited your search to very small topic area and then hardly got any information at all, or you had to wade through a pile of boring stuff. Jack chose the latter method, since usually she had plenty of wading time.

It seemed like the big news was still the hardware theft in Brugges. Jack scanned a couple of the entries and got the impression that the reason it was getting so much attention was that there had been a lot of vandalism in the theft. All the cases in one server room had been literally ripped open, the disk pulled out leaving behind an unbelievable mess. It was a 'Man Bites Dog' story for sure, since even though theft was common enough, usually thieves took great pains to be discreet. The whole point was to make it take as long as possible for the theft to be discovered, so that the logs for the time of the crime would have been destroyed. Such a blatant display was so rare Jack could never recall an incident like it.

Beautiful Red

There was, of course, no end to the speculation on the nets about why this had happened. Some suspected streeters, others opined that a revolutionary group of anti-progress activists were making a political statement. Some thought that it was a regular theft gone wrong, perhaps interrupted. Jack took all these opinions with the weight they ought to have — very little — and headed over to a board created entirely by intelligent agents.

There was still plenty of debate about intelligent agents, the name assigned to smart computer programs. They were kind of hard to define; one common denominator was that they were smart enough to pass the Turing test, though that piece of trivia only scratched the surface. Some people were concerned that they would achieve sentience and then all hell would break loose, mostly those people were labeled "anti-progress," though that was really an unfair characterization. The truth was that no one knew what would happen if a program became self aware, but the economic value of intelligent agents was undeniable, so they were common enough.

There were plenty of tasks they couldn't perform — anything requiring subtlety, intuition, diplomacy or outright deception. But for logical analysis they couldn't be beat and they were fast and tireless. Whether you could rightly call their assessments "opinions" was a matter of debate, but Jack wanted to read something other than political rhetoric disguised as analysis. She paged over to IA Security News Log, a site of "opinion" pieces by off-duty intelligent agents working in security. Jack had met Adrian on their companion board for what they jokingly (everyone hoped) called unintelligent agents.

Jack ran a search for the Brugges theft and came up with a few articles. One pointed out that humanity had a history of illogical actions and this latest example was no stranger than someone getting in a fist fight under a surveillance camera, an all too common occurrence. Another article focussed on the cost benefit analysis, the payoff versus risk of apprehension. That agent argued that for a person with sufficient motivation, the risk of leaving evidence and possibly being caught was lower than the possible benefits. Another poster, particularly well known for its provocative remarks, reiterated its usual refrain that humans were morons.

Jack didn't find a lot of new information there, but the aggregate of all she had read definitely explained the incident's noteworthiness. Who would be sufficiently motivated to steal disk when you could just buy it off any streeter? Jack knew that streeters didn't earn enough from the wares they sold to make a theft like that worthwhile. It was an interesting problem and made a good diversion from the problem still on Jack's mind — why was someone using corporate systems to cover their tracks on the nets?

She wondered if the incidents were connected in some way. She suspected that she was just grasping at straws and seeing patterns where none existed, but they were both unusual and seemingly illogical incidents. Jack almost hoped there was a connection, even though that would make the problem even more intractable. She shook her head and checked the time.

Ugh, she thought. It was mid-afternoon already and she had gotten only a few hours sleep the night before, waking in the middle of the night to go on her break and enter mission. She knew she was over tired, but didn't want to sleep. She looked out the widow and saw that the day was moderately bright and figured that a walk wouldn't hurt. She changed her clothes, grabbed her non-uniform jacket and left the apartment.

She walked out of her building and turned left instead of right like she would if she were going to the train stop. She walked along the sidewalk, not really looking where she was going, just walking. She passed a few streeters and regular folks coming or going to work. The street was like any other, lined with tall buildings of housing units, some of the nicer ones with shops or cafes in their ground floors. A few private enclosed vehicles hovered through the street, but mostly the street was used by people on scooters, as there weren't many reasons to be in this neighbourhood for people rich enough to own a car. Most people were on foot, though, heading to or from a train stop.

Jack watched the other people moving purposely through the street. Everyone looked so intent, so focussed, and Jack realized that she usually did the same. Most people were online almost all the time and walking toward a train stop or to a store was just something for their bodies to do. It was as if the physical body were merely a transportation device for the mind, just a way of getting to one physical location from another.

As Jack looked at her surroundings more closely, she started noticing things she had never seen before, having always been online. The boring similarity of all the buildings, for example. Even her own building, which she loved for its antiquated wooden door, was essentially the same 20 story glass and platinum monolith as every other building she passed.

Even the people were eerily alike, with their vacant plugged in stares, fashionable bodies and faces, uniforms or corporate approved dress code outfits. Jack stopped and looked at her reflection in the mirrored window of the building next to her. She knew she wasn't as fashionable as most of the other people on the street; she couldn't be bothered to get a new face every year and she while she went through a phase when she was younger of going through several body types, she finally found one that felt right and just kept it. Even her hair colour had remained the same since she was a teenager — she now bought number 772 (sapphire) by the wholesale case.

She supposed that she had always had a slightly rebellious streak with her appearance. Almost all her implants were subdermal; the only exception was a small stainless stud beneath her lower lip which she got at the age of twelve, in an adolescent attempt to look like everyone else. She had to admit that she still liked the way it looked, somewhat striking against her otherwise unadulterated skin. She once toyed with the idea of getting tattoo-skin, a programmable layer just under the epidermis that could render any image, but she had never bothered and now it was so common that hardly anyone who had it used it for more than changing skin colour.

So she looked young but out of date, with a compact body just shy of 1.7 metres tall. Today, she wore loose pants of a dark strong material that ended mid calf and draped over her knee high boots. Her shirt was made of an iridescent material that had been popular six months previously; Jack liked it because just over her breasts was a red flashing 12:00, a symbol of technological incompetence that was the unofficial logo of the loose group of security pros that gathered on the IAs' human board. As a top layer she wore a hip length black shiny jacket with eighteen pockets so cleverly built into it that an observer would never know there were any pockets at all. After looking at herself for a full minute, as if she were a stranger, Jack decided she was pleased with her appearance, even though she would never be singled out in a crowd and asked how she did it.

OOOIO

OKAY, MAYBE I have been being a touch melodramatic about this memory problem. I have done a little research now and I think it may be some kind of brain problem, but nothing serious. Most likely it's an artifact of one of the new implants. Blackouts supposedly are a symptom of incorrectly calibrated wetware connections. It's uncommon, but it happens.

I've decided to go to the upgrade salon tomorrow and see if the people there have heard anything about this side effect. I can't find anything on their boards, but they don't like to advertise their problems, so hopefully I can just get a replacement or something. I hope I won't have to spend a lot of time in installation, but this needs to be fixed. I can't go on like this - I'm tired all the time and I'm starting to worry about what's happening during the time I'm unable to remember.

Just to be safe, I have turned on automatic recording. Even limiting it to audio, this is going to take up a huge chunk of memory, no irony intended, but at least I'll be able to hear what I've been doing in those lapses.

I think the smartest thing I've done in the last little while is taking the mood stabilizers. I was starting to really go off the rails there. Looking back, I'm surprised no one has turned me in to the crazy police. The way I had been acting before the stabilizers, anyone would have thought I was some kind of lunatic.

SIX

JACK STARTED WALKING back to her apartment, planning her next move. If she could trace the path of the unknown login back from the Bellis system, she may be able to find out where it originated. If she could find where it came from, she might be able to figure out what they were doing. She was pretty confident that whoever it was and wherever it came from, the Bellis system was not the final destination. There were no flags raised by the security system and, as far as anyone could tell, no damage done aside from the downtime the other day.

Jack also wanted to play with her new toys and she came up with an idea that she hoped would be a cross between a gritty crime vidcast and an urban documentary. She walked a few blocks away from her building to a darker area more heavily populated by streeters. She saw no uniformed security goons and for once didn't look at the situation as a potential training exercise. Instead, she felt compelled to watch the streeters themselves. She looked at them as if for the first time, as if she were a tourist and they were novel and interesting scenery. She was accustomed to seeing them only as a potential threat or source of some grey market bargain. More often than not, Jack, like everyone else, didn't even notice them.

This particular street had many unauthorized dwellings — everything from packing boxes, holo-tents and piles of blankets were being used to mark out where one person's territory ended and someone else's began. By the circulation of goods and the permanence of some of the encampments, Jack saw that many of the streeters had clearly been living this way for some time, but there were a some who had the look of someone who was fairly new to street life. There

were a few indicators — some were wearing tattered uniforms as opposed to well patched generic items and they seemed to have a wild
and afraid look rather than the resigned attitude of someone who
has seen pretty much all of what the street had to offer.

Jack approached an alley that was well known to be a popular
scrounging ground for streeters. There was a mid range upgrades
store in the building, whose staff often discarded unfashionable
items that the streeters could use or sell. Also, the alley was fairly
well sheltered and it appeared that many of the new people were
staying close to it. Jack stood at the mouth of the alley, looked
around and saw that there were not too many people nearby and
those who were there were preoccupied with their own concerns.
She fished in one of her pockets and grabbed a couple of the micro
recorders. She quickly rolled them one at a time down the alley, then
abruptly turned and headed back to her building.

Partly she just wanted to see how well the recorders worked, but
partly she was genuinely interested in seeing the streeters' lives. The
popular boards had been full of prurient tales of streeter crime and
degradation and Jack suspected it was mostly propaganda to keep
people from helping them. Still, she thought it would make for interesting watching. All her life she had done some of her best thinking while watching video, so she hoped that this might be a good
diversion as she worked out the path of the mystery visitors to the
Buyside and Bellis systems.

Back in her apartment she brought up the recorders' software
and activated the units she had left in the alley. At first she was
thrown by their fly-eyes multiple view of the scene, but she quickly
learned how to isolate individual views or start a three dimensional
view. In the 3D view it was uncanny how lifelike the scene felt. It was
exactly as if she were standing near the northern wall about a third
of the way in. She could turn around and look up or down like normal and see everything as if she were there. She could hear audio in
three dimensions also; an airbus screeching overhead prompted her
to look up and the subtle change in sound felt entirely realistic. The
only thing that was missing was smell and touch. And of course, she
was rooted to the spot. It was eerie and fascinating.

She paged out of the three-dimensional mode and set up a series
of individual views to run in the background while she worked. She
set them to her left eye, her usual choice for secondary input. She

put on the coffee and heated a meal packet and called up all the information she had about the intrusion. She pulled up the list of addresses used — the incoming address from Buyside and the outgoing address at Bellis, as well as the tools she had found on the scene at Buyside's Client Delivery System.

She started to look at the tools by reading the code directly, not expecting to learn anything explicitly, more just to get a feel for her quarry. She found you could often tell a bit about a person or group by the code they wrote. As she was scanning the lines of text and symbols, her attention was drawn to one of the images from the micro recorders. It looked like a scheduled dump of castoffs from the upgrade station was about to occur, since a small group of streeters had gathered in the alley and seemed to be waiting.

The group seemed to be mostly veterans, a few faces Jack recognized from the neighbourhood. She suspected that, like in most ad hoc communities, the old timers got the pick of the goods and the newbies had to salvage what they could from the sloppy seconds. Jack noticed a few obvious newbies, one who stuck out particularly. He had the same age appearance as Jack and looked like he was wearing a corporate uniform, though it had certainly seen better days. His appearance wasn't what made him stand out from the crowd, though, it was more his behaviour.

The other streeters were all vying for a position around the hatch at the back of the store, while simultaneously trying to maintain control over whatever goods or other belongings they had with them. This streeter had no items with him at all, which was unusual, and he stood some distance from the others. He didn't participate in the light conversation or arguments the others were engaged in; in fact he almost looked as if he were involved in some terribly interesting activity online — he had the vacant stare, the slack jaw and the lack of apparent interest in the goings on of the alley. Jack thought was odd how a behaviour that is appropriate in most circumstances for someone with a job and money was entirely strange and even a bit disturbing in another context.

There was no point in playing with the micro recorders if she didn't fully test them, so she switched the view to three dimensions. She felt a strange lack of equilibrium as it appeared to her that the alley materialized around her. She could see and hear the action as if she were right there and she found she had a strong desire to hide, which of course simply reinforced the other bizarre feeling of being unable to move. The reality of the sounds and moving images combined with the artifact of being rooted to one spot was, Jack discovered, quite unnerving.

Things got even more strange when the hatch in the back of the building opened and the action began. Various items of hardware — diodes, implants, disk, transistors, wireless nodes, whatever — came dropping out of the hatch into the large grey bin in the alley. The majority of the streeters mobbed the bin, but in a very orderly fashion. As Jack had noticed earlier, the more experienced streeters somehow managed to find themselves at the right place to get the prime items, while the others had to sift through the remainders to look for the salvageable objects. Jack looked at the unusual man, not entirely surprised to see that he seemed to not even have noticed that the action had begun.

All of a sudden, though, he seemed to come to life, sputtering about the mouth and lurching forward toward the group. Jack involuntarily tried to jump back and was momentarily struck by a feeling of terror when she found herself unable to move. She quickly remembered that she was really just watching a clever film, but her physical fear was difficult to control. The man lumbered into the fray of other people around the bin and completely disregarding what appeared to be the mores of the situation, plunged both arms into the bin. He threw the uninteresting items out of the bin and into the crowd, while literally pulling apart larger items to get at the more valuable parts inside. He stuffed the parts he wanted into his pockets and scattered the crowd with his flailing arms and flying detritus.

When he had finished amassing his collection, he walked straight through the stunned crowd and headed out of the alley. He was walking straight toward the micro recorder that Jack was monitoring, so she had a clear view of his face. He was wearing the same thousand metre stare he had before, as if he were online. He lumbered toward Jack, who reflexively recoiled as he approached, when it seemed as if he walked through her as he stepped over the micro recorder. Jack turned to watch him go, as did the other streeters. Jack was still watching his retreating back when the other streeters regained their composure and began sorting through the items he had left behind.

Jack finally disconnected from the recorder and found herself sitting at her table in a similar physical state as she had been after her break and enter at the Buyside system. What the hell was that? She couldn't recall ever seeing anything like it. It was as if that man were not paying any attention at all to his actions. Jack admitted that a lack of attention to the physical world was a fairly common occurrence, but not when someone was actually doing something physical. It was easier to pay partial attention to the network while being almost fully engaged in the real world than it was to go the other way.

Thinking about what she saw, if she imagined the same behaviour in a system, Jack would have identified the man as a bot — clearly not in control of his actions, not having any agency of his own. But he was definitely a human, unless military cybernetics had advanced dramatically and in complete secrecy and they had unleashed their android creations on the street. They could only manage two of the three, at best, Jack thought and chuckled.

She searched a few boards for any information that might help and found a discussion on a few similar sightings elsewhere. There were a few still pictures of people who looked similar enough to the man Jack saw in the alley. They weren't always with other streeters, but they always looked completely vacant and were either stealing or destroying gear. Jack posted a brief description of what she had seen and included an excerpt of the video. Some of the other posters immediately asked questions about the incident and she discussed the scene with them for some time. There were the usual mix of theories, none of which appealed to Jack. She couldn't help thinking of the scene in terms of a system. He was just a bot. Nothing out of the ordinary there. Except that he was a human, not a program.

Jack paged out of the board and went offline. She was disturbed by what she had seen and she needed to compose herself. She got herself a beer and some toast and focussed on those very corporeal tasks of eating and drinking. After the toast was gone and the beer was halfway there, she still felt at odds and needed something else to help ground her. She opened up her fridge and pulled out the peas. She lit a frozen cigarette and spent the next ten minutes forcing herself into a more relaxed state, while simultaneously increasing her heat rate and general nervous system activity.

She sat, smoking and drinking and began to review the tools used by the Buyside intruder. She started to read the code, looking for similarities between the programs. She first compared the part of the "map" to the document she had obtained from Gilles. After searching through the full document, she found the snippet embedded within it. Clearly, the document she was using and the document used by the intruder were identical. No great surprise here, since the spec was obviously easily available.

After ruling out this piece of code from being a useful clue, she turned to the other two pieces of code. She scanned them both for comments and similarities in style. She looked for particular designs and peculiar methods. She found very few similarities and determined that the tools had separate original authors. However, the code represented by the two by four had clearly been modified from its original condition. A chunk had been added in the middle and this part was written in a similar style to the other script. Jack copied the added lines and looked at them along with the other code. She recognized a style which had been popular a few years ago among pacific rim crackers, a particular way of laying out the code designed to make it more readable. She also recognized artifacts of a scripting language that had never attained much popularity outside the rim.

It was a legitimate clue, but to a certain extent knowing that the intruder had code from the rim was sort of like knowing that burglars had gloves from a particular mid sized franchise. It made Jack feel like she was making progress even though it didn't actually narrow things down at all. Jack decided instead to focus on the address logs. She knew that it was theoretically possible to construct a path from the information in the logs about the intruder. She had learned in her security history courses that before the ability of the everywherenet to essentially track all movement on the network, security professionals had been forced to track the paths of stealthy crackers. Jack looked up their tactics and tried to apply them to her current situation.

She didn't have a lot to go by — some residual entry information that she acquired at the Buyside end and entry and exit information from the Bellis eastern system. She ran them through the various algorithms she had found on the nets that had been used in the past and came up with a startling result — the origin of the intruder was from another network. They came from outside everywherenet.

Until that moment, Jack hadn't known that there even were networks outside everywherenet. Why would anyone bother, when everyone and everything was hooked up together? If privacy were the concern, there were plenty of encryption solutions to that problem and everywherenet was built specifically to allow transparency with privacy. The cost and complexity of building your own network would be prohibitive, Jack figured and even if it weren't it was simply redundant.

Even more shocking was that the intruders entered into the common network from a landline. It appeared that their entry point hacked into the network somewhere in a major city, though Jack couldn't tell which one. The logs showed only that it was a MetropolisGroup access point, which was the name given to the everywherenet subcommittee of the major uberurban firms. The tap could have originated in any of the massive cities and then it seemed to bounce from corporate intranet to corporate intranet until it found its final destination. And that destination was also pretty strange — it appeared to be a private citizen.

Jack called up a directory and map. She quickly located this person, one Estella Rowan, at an address in a city in Europe and, on a not very well-thought out whim, pinged her. Jack had no idea what she would say if her query was answered, but the point was moot. There was no response. She wasn't particularly surprised; most people didn't respond to pings from strangers. When personal systems were first becoming popular, spammers switched from messaging addresses to pinging individuals directly. Almost everyone had some kind of blocker to avoid unwanted communications.

Jack looked at the information she had on hand and wondered how she had missed it. Estella Rowan lived in Brugges. The same city in the Benelux where there had been a strange theft of hardware recently. Jack was convinced there had to be a connection, though she couldn't see what it might be. She ran a search for an update on the Brugges robbery, but came up with nothing. Then she ran a search on Estella Rowan from Brugges.

Bingo.

SEVEN

JACK SCANNED A news report from the previous day. "Estella Rowan, a 63-year old adult entertainer, was reported missing yesterday by her employer after she failed to log in at work for her shift that evening." Jack felt a slight chill as she realized that the evening in question was the night of the Brugges robbery. The reports were not connecting the events — surely Brugges had its share of crime and what would a prostitute have to do with a theft of electronic parts? Jack connected the events, though. The theft had occurred only three quarters of an hour after Rowan's system had been accessed. Jack had to try and find Rowan, who might be able to lead her to the people who had contacted the missing woman just before the heist.

Jack cracked her knuckles and settled into her chair. She pulled up her home brew three dimensional graphic representation of everywherenet and followed the path she estimated that the intruders had taken after they left the Bellis system. It felt a lot like the good old days, when she had first begun work on the 3D system and Jack felt herself fall into the old groove. She had spent many a long night slipping through the tiny passages and crooked labyrinths of various networks, many of which she really had no right to wander. The old thrill returned, though now she had age and experience behind her. It somehow didn't seem to make that much difference.

She saw herself sliding through what appeared as green glowing tubes, individual packets represented by lighter green dots. She moved with the dots up, down and around the snaking interconnected pipes. After a few moments, it felt like walking through the neighbourhood where she lived. To be truly honest, it was easier.

Jack knew the networks as if she'd lived there all her life, which, in a way, she had.

She arrived at the representation of Rowan, a nicely painted wooden door, and Jack knew the woman would be offline — it's pretty hard to be missing if you are broadcasting your position to everyone on the 'nets. Jack pictured herself delicately knocking at Rowan's door, her own system pinging Rowan's offline system in a way that could force her online if the configuration files were set for emergency access. Of course, that didn't work. Certainly the authorities had tried that route already and failed. Still, Jack was a firm believer in trying the simplest solution first — her experience as a programmer had taught her that.

She mentally regrouped and set about attacking the problem differently. She found one of her professional tools that was represented as a shimmering key. It was essentially a lock pick for various types of systems. She set it to work and watched as it conformed itself to the inner shape of the lock. Eventually it glowed green and appeared to resolve itself into a solid shape. Jack took hold of it and turned. The lock opened and the door swung slowly inward.

Rowan's system was pictured as a large house, the kind almost no one actually lived in anymore. Jack found herself in the foyer and could see into a large parlour that was obviously used only for entertaining. The doors to the private rooms of the home were closed and Jack knew they would be locked. She didn't want to open them, knowing that such a breach was highly illegal, but more importantly Jack couldn't justify doing to someone else something she would hate to have done to her. So she contented herself with poking around the more public areas of Rowan's system.

The public address was on display above the door and some other basic contact information could be found by looking around the place. Rowan's place of employment, the Shadow Room, was listed along with its address on a list of public contacts tacked to a bulletin board near the door. Her calendar of public engagements was also available there, as well as a few publicity images of her body she probably used for work.

Rowan was an attractive and trendy looking woman, if the publicity shots were to be believed. She had short spiky iridescent hair that gave her face a look that was both intense and soft at the same time. She looked youthful, with no visible wrinkles on her dark brown skin. She had also clearly had her hands enhanced, as the fingers appeared slightly longer and more slender than would have looked natural. She was, of course, naked in most the shots and often bent into a contortionist's pose. In the few images where she was dressed, she wore very fashionable dresses of light flowing and almost translucent material. Jack looked at the photos for a long time, as if the images would tell her something about the woman other than how to pick her out of a lineup.

Eventually, Jack moved into the parlour, but found little of interest in there. Rowan clearly didn't have many visitors to her system and Jack suspected that her business transactions would occur over the Shadow Room's network for security reasons. Jack guessed Rowan didn't have many friends, since it was her employer who reported her missing and there was no evidence that anyone had been here in recent times. Jack checked the guestbook and saw that Rowan herself hadn't even accessed this part of the system in over two months. Jack wondered what her own public space looked like, wondering how similar she and the missing woman might be.

Jack had decided that she could not justify breaking the locks into Rowan's private space, but she felt compelled to approach the doors anyway. She touched the door off the parlour and let out a tiny yelp as it swung open. Jack staggered back and fell on to the settee in a thump. She could see into a kitchen-type area and was shocked by what she saw.

It looked like a cyclone had torn through the room. Furniture was upended, the wallpaper was torn from the walls in great strips, holes were gouged in the walls and floor. Jack was torn between a desire to go offline immediately and a strong sense of curiosity that begged her to investigate. She moved cautiously to the door and called Estella Rowan's name loudly.

"Hello!" she shouted into the wreckage. "Is anyone here?" She stayed in the doorway. "My name is Jack. I'm a Security Officer Class 5. I'm here to help." She felt like an idiot. There were no signs of life inside and although it went against every nerve in her body and any sense of ethics she had, Jack stepped over the threshold and entered Estella's mind.

The disaster area that was once represented as a kitchen was a maelstrom of destroyed items. Jack stepped carefully through the rubble, looking for anything that might leave a clue about what had happened. She couldn't even imagine what this meant — a mental breakdown, some sort of catastrophic software meltdown; Jack was just grasping at straws trying to make sense of this situation.

She continued to call out in the hopes that Estella would answer, though she was beginning to fear that there wasn't anyone there, which was a frightening concept. Integrated systems ran off the electrical current generated by the human body and therefore would shut down when the body died. It seemed that the system was working perfectly well, even if it was in some sort of horrendously broken format. Estella must be alive, but there seemed to be no sign of consciousness inside.

Jack sifted through the rubble, finding broken china, holes in the walls and nothing whatsoever indicating what had happened. It could have been a fight, vandalism, some other kind of upheaval. Jack realized that the kitchen wasn't going to answer any questions and she would have to look further in the house if she was going to learn anything.

She stepped up to the kitchen door and timidly pushed it forward. It creaked open and Jack saw a continuation of the mess she was standing in. It was a living area that was actually used for living and it was strewn with books, clothes and equipment. Almost everything was broken or ripped and Jack got the sense that it was destroyed in two stages — the first being some kind of a conflict and the second being blind rage. The way things were thrown around and pushed away from their usual places indicated a fight or perhaps showed the path of someone trying to escape from the room. But the vandalism could not have been a natural side effect, it had to have been deliberate.

Jack could see, however, a slight path in the rubble. She followed the trail of fallen lamps and ripped curtains to another door. She cracked it open and saw a bedroom, in the same state of disarray as the rest of the house. The mattress was pulled off the bed and tossed aside, after having been torn open. Jack thought there must have been pillows once, judging from the piles of poly-filler on the floor. The path she was following continued through the pillow wreckage. Jack followed the trail, which was becoming more obvious now, to a closet door.

She pulled it open and at first couldn't comprehend what she was looking at. There was little other then the haircut and skin tone that connected the mess in the closet with the woman in the images Jack had been studying in the foyer. The body was bloody and battered, though on closer inspection it was definitely Rowan. She looked as if she had been at the losing end of a fistfight with a knife salesman and Jack leant in closer to look at the wounds. She felt her heart nearly stop as the body moved, twitching and staggering, and fell on top of her.

Jack screamed and flailed at the woman, who moaned and writhed, but did not fight back. Her body was almost completely slack, except for some twitching and drooling which caused Jack to panic even more. Jack was strong, but she could not budge the weight trapping her. Every time she shoved, Rowan would make a horrible noise and another body part, slick with blood, would rub against Jack, trapping her further. Just as panic threatened to cause her to lose consciousness, Jack remembered that she was in a simulation.

She quickly switched to code view, caught her breath and fought the gorge rising in her throat. She slowly regained her composure, but couldn't stop shaking. She felt as if she could still feel the blood on her body, though she was dry except for her own sweat. She scanned the code, trying to forget the image of the pretty woman in the photos turned into the vacant, corpse-like thing that she had recently encountered.

She forced herself to focus on reading the code and recognized the signature of a human consciousness, but never like she had seen it before. She copied a random sampling of the code and searched for a similar pattern on the nets. All of the hits she brought up were medical articles discussing comatose patients and a few classified documents. Jack scanned the medical papers and matched the pattern of the code she had taken from Estella as similar to the brain pattern of people who were in long term comas.

This made sense; if Estella were in a coma, her system would be unable to respond to pinging and there wouldn't be any activity. The coma theory didn't explain the mess, though and it certainly didn't answer where she was physically. Jack checked the sources of the classified documents. They were branded ESA; the European Security Agency. Jack knew she didn't have the skills to get access to them. She wondered if there was another way.

She switched programs and called up her three dimensional museum interface. She walked past the welcome desk and coat check, past Greco-Roman friezes, Rodin's sculpture The Kiss, Kirschov's holo-painting Sunlight and other priceless masterpieces and found herself in front of the Escher. She spoke a few words of command and soon heard the chime of notification at the other end.

>Adrian, you there?
>>Hey, yeah, I'm here. Long time no chat. What's up?
>Plenty. I'm switching to double encryption, okay?
>>Now I'm really interested. Okay. Key 73?
>Seven three.

Jack selected double encryption and pulled up her key number 39. Long ago, Jack and Adrian had agreed that if they ever had to discuss keys, they would use a number in the clear that they would translate to a different number using a simple mathematical formula they could do manually (add five, divide by two). It wouldn't make a big difference to a dedicated attacker, but it made things more difficult for everyday eavesdroppers.

Once the encryption was loaded, Jack reloaded the channel.

>Hey Adrian?
>>I'm here. So, spill the goodies!
>I got embroiled in something at the office which started off being a not so run of the mill intruder and has ended up with a missing woman who may be in physical danger. The trouble is, pretty much none of it is any of my official business and I have shit for authorization for any of it.
>>Cool.
>Kind of. Mostly it's just wacky now. I'm trying to figure out what happened to this woman and all I've got is a live log from her consciousness. I ran a search of the code from the log and came up with some classified documents from the ESA.
>>A ha!
>Yeah.
>>So you were wondering if I had any inside poop for you.
>Yup. I know you have access to that stuff from some of your posts on the blinking twelves. I don't need to see the docs, I just want to know how this girl's brain patterns connect with their stuff. It could just be references to comas, which is the only other stuff I could find that matched.
>>...
>>Were you planning on telling me about this little adventure if you hadn't needed my help?
>(sigh)I'm sorry, A. It started off being just work, you know, and I didn't want to share it, really. It was fun and I hadn't had an adventure in so

long. And then, next thing I know it's a day later and I'm in some
chick's brain and it's just totally out of control and...
>>Whoa, J. It's cool. Just be cool.
>Sorry. It's been a fucked up...

Jack glanced at the time and nearly had a fit. It had been nearly
twenty-four hours since she got up and that was after only a few
hours sleep.

>Sorry. It's been a fucked up 40 hours or so.
>>Jesus, you sound like a wreck.
>I am a wreck. I need sleep.
>>Okay. Send me the code and I'll see what I can do.
>Thanks, A. Really, I mean I really appreciate...
>>Aw, can the crap, J. Just get some zees and I'll talk to you in nine
or ten hours. Same channel, okay?
>Sounds great, A. Thanks.
>>No worries. Catch you later.

Adrian broke the connection and Jack went offline. She ran her
hands over her face and realized that she had been running on nothing but adrenaline. She shucked her clothes on the floor, not even
bothering to stuff them in the autoclave. She had a quick shower,
blew off and clambered into bed. She fell asleep to fitful dreams of
being alternately trapped under the corpse of Estella Rowan and being chased through the glowing green corridors of the network by an
unseen force and through it all she kept seeing the recurring image
of the dazed face of the man in the streeters' alley.

OOOII

THE UPGRADE SALON was worse than useless. Those idiots don't know their asses from holes in the ground. I start to describe my symptoms and the animated mannequin that works the front counter just cocks his cute little head and says, "Gee, I've never heard of that. Maybe you should visit a psi doctor," then goes back to talking with his stupid co-idiot about their fingernails or something.

Fuck him and his fashionable little nails. A psi doctor. As if those quacks are going to help me. I'm not suffering from delusions of insignificance or something, I'm fucking losing my memory for chrissakes. Now I don't know what to do. Son of a bitch.

EIGHT

JACK WOKE ON her own sometime near noon the next day. She felt like crap and was sure she looked like it too. She fired up the coffee machine and dug out a breakfast bar. She stirred her coffee with the bar, trying to get some moisture and extra caffeine into the nutrient laden brick. She cracked her neck and picked up her clothes from where she had dropped them the previous night. She put them on, even though there were clean clothes in the autoclave. She just couldn't be bothered to open up the hatch and she didn't think she would be leaving the apartment any time soon.

She idly ate her breakfast and drank her coffee, thinking about the events of the past couple of days. In the hazy light of midday, she thought she could see similarities between the man in the alley and the representation of Estella Rowan she had encountered in her system. Jack realized that systemic representations were flawed in many ways — she knew it better than most, having written several — but she couldn't help but think that the look on Estella's face when Jack found her in the closet was eerily similar to that of the man in the alley. She called up the video from the alley and zoomed in on his face as he was coming toward her when he left the alley. The lack of expression, the muscles so completely slack, was identical to the way Estella Rowan looked before Jack left the representation. She found it hard to believe that the two events could be unrelated.

She fired up her interface and saw that she had a message from Adrian asking her to get in contact. Jack opened up the double en-crypted messenger and, using the same key as the day before, sent a request to Adrian. Shortly she received a response.

>Hey, J. Good news. Switch to 17?
>>17. Okay.

Jack broke the connection and established a new one using her eleventh key. Adrian soon joined the channel.

>You get some sleep, there?
>>Yeah, finally. I just got up.
>Good deal. I've got some info for you.
>>Thanks. What's the scoop?
>I got a perfect match between your sample and the ESA docs.
>>Now that's interesting. I was sort of hoping for and against that. What else can you tell me?
>The docs in question were reports of experiments done about remote control of cybernetic bio-organisms.
>>Uh, okay. Sounds disturbing.
>The subjects in this project were bonobo chimpanzees, if that makes you feel better.
>>Not really, but at least the mental image is different. Can you give me some specifics?
>I guess. I shouldn't, really. These are classified docs... but what the hell. I read the docs and your matching sample comes from analysis of the brainwaves of the bonobos after the programmed instructions had been sent.
>>Can you be more specific about these programmed instructions?
>Looks like they were trying to see if you could use your typical wetware brain/machine interface to make a bio-organism do things, as opposed to just receive data. You know, force our chimp cousins to walk in a circle, not eat the food, whatever.
>>Okay. Sort of high tech, specialized brainwashing.
>Pretty much. The sample you sent me matched the measure of brain patterns when the subjects were being fully controlled by the programming.
>>Yikes.
>Oh yeah, the experiments were wildly successful. The trouble was that the subjects became entirely dependent on the programs, so there was no going back to a natural state after.
>>Somehow, that doesn't surprise me.
>...
>>...
>So, you said you found this pattern in a human, is that right?
>>Yup. I took a copy of it out of her personal system myself.
>God. This report ended with recommendations to ban the use of this technology on any bio-organism, human or other.
>>I can see why. It was pretty horrible in there.
>I'm not surprised. The docs were pretty explicit. It seems that the bonobos all tried to fight the program as it was making its way into their consciousnesses.

>>When I was in her system, it was such a mess that it looked like a fight had occurred in there. I couldn't figure out how that would happen, but this makes sense.
>Yeah. They all fought and they all lost. And the really horrible part is that it took days.
>>Oh, god.
>Days of fighting and this slow inevitable descent into a stupor. They were slavering automatons at the end, Jack. They all had to be killed.
>>Christ.
>It was one of the worst things I've seen. The docs had video of the whole ordeal. Be thankful I'm not passing that on.
>>God, I am. Thanks for finding it for me, A. I'm really sorry you had to see it all, though.
>Me, too. I just feel for that woman. And I have to wonder who is doing this. The ESA docs claim they destroyed all copies of the program they used.
>>For fuck's sake, everyone knows you can't destroy code. Someone will have made a backup somewhere, someone always does. And then it's in the nets and it's in the world forever.
>I know. No one ever learns. But that doesn't answer the next question.
>>Which is?
>What are you going to do now?
>>God, A., I dunno. Track down whoever's doing this, I guess.
>She had a job didn't she? Why not go to the authorities?
>>... You're kidding, right?
>Yeah. I guess. After what you've done, they're more likely to lock you up than look into this.
>>I know. Crap, I never should have pursued this.
>Hey, you were whining about things being boring.
>>I know.
>There's an old saying where I'm from: Be careful what you wish for, it might be a goat.
>>(laughter) Thanks for the advice, A.
>Hey, better late than never. You flash if you need any more help, okay?
>>Thanks.
>Be careful.
>>Will do. Later.
>Later.

Jack disconnected and shook her head in shock. She was afraid that Estella had been violated in some way, but was leaning more toward the idea that it was a physical assault which had led to a mental breakdown of some sort. That there was some way to fix it if she could just find her physical whereabouts. Now she wasn't even sure if it was worth trying to track down her body. This was all getting to be too much. She was just a Security Officer Class 5. She wasn't really equipped for this.

She lay down on her bed, still wearing yesterday's clothes and thought about crying. She wasn't much of a weeper and the tears didn't come, even though she thought it might make her feel better. Some kind of release of the tension. She thought about sex. One of her usual partners would certainly be available if Jack just went on-line and asked, but she couldn't bring herself to find someone when she was in the midst of all this horror. She finally just screamed into her pillow, beating it with her fists and tearing at her sheets.

She finished beating up her bed after about two or three minutes and collapsed among the rumpled sheets. Without even thinking about it, she fell asleep. When she woke, only a few minutes had passed, but Jack felt more able to cope with the situation. She got up and sheepishly straightened her bed. She changed into clean clothes and decided to get ready to do something. She still had a day and a half before she had to be back at work and she was filled with a sense of obligation to solve this problem. She owed it to Adrian who had risked serious trouble with several versions of the cops to get the information Jack needed and she owed it to Estella Rowan. Jack got down to work.

• • •

She meticulously picked apart the code left behind by the intruders at Buyside, running every individual line through the nets looking for possible authors. She followed the path of the intrusion back to the other end, the originating end, hypothesizing and guessing where there were gaps in the information. She cross referenced, indexed, filled in the blanks and made progress. Eventually she narrowed it down to a shadowy group called variously the Red, the Society for Creative Anarchicism and nowherenet, depending on the part of the world. They had been blamed for various incidents in many municipalities and corporations, many of which were illegal in some jurisdictions, but there didn't seem to be any coherent understanding of their goals.

They were generally not perceived as a significant threat since most of their actions were harmless to property and people other than themselves. They were really more like pranksters, although a few of their actions had spiralled out of control and caused damage or injury. They were, however, mocked and vilified by the corporate press, since their mandate seemed to be to do whatever fucked up the status quo. They picketed offices, staged performance art installations at upgrade salons, subverted networking with frivolous messages. When they had a message, it was vaguely anti-technology and pro-physicality, but more often than not they seemed to be causing trouble for the sheer bloody mindedness of it all.

Jack had to admit that she couldn't recall having heard of them before. She had never personally encountered one of their "actions" and she was not a good consumer of the corporate press. She deleted the Bellis propaganda email unread and she rarely sought out any of the big corporate boards. She preferred to get her news from real people, whose agendas were obvious and whose pockets were shallow. Since this group tended to converge on the large firms, their shenanigans didn't make the news outlets Jack frequented.

She hit all the big corp boards now, though, running searches for all the monikers she had found for the group. There wasn't a lot to report and most of it was so full of vitriol and ideology that it left Jack with more sympathy for the perpetrators than the so-called victims. Then she thought of Estella and the sympathy died in her heart. She turned to the opposite side, the underground cracker boards. She had always participated in these boards, the ones that drew those people who skirted and sometimes bodily crossed the line between legality and illegality. At one time she was a heavy contributor to the community and she had built up enough of reputation under her first net handle that she was regarded as an insider. She could nose around without arousing too much suspicion.

She switched identities and brought up one of the more edgy communities. She made small talk for some time, catching up old acquaintances and getting current with the gossip. She spent almost three quarters of an hour just chatting with the group before dropping hints about the SCA, nowherenet and the Red. Mostly, the group found them to be at best a humorous diversion and at worst a problem for serious crackers in the image department. But after a few hours of conversation, she came away with a real live lead. An address in a nearby city.

Jack paged out of the cracker boards and disconnected. A physical address. They might not be the exact people she was looking for, but they would have to do. Jack fired up her system again and booked a ticket out of town. She packed a small bag with essentials

— her toothbrush, a fresh pair of underpants, a handful of micro recorders and a sonic self-defender she had acquired through another impulse purchase from one of the streeters by her apartment. She left a notice in her apartment's systems that if she had not returned within twenty-four hours, to notify Adrian and Gilles simultaneously but separately.

She left specific messages for each of them. She didn't really think that either of them could help her if she got into real trouble and she certainly didn't expect them to finish off her mission, as that was what it had now become. She just realized that they were the only ones who had any idea what she was up to and that they might care what happened to her. So they ought to know if something happened.

She stepped out of her apartment and stood on the threshold looking back. It really was a pitiful little room. The window looked over the street into the window of an identical little room in an identical building. The occupant of that room was rarely in and when she was, she kept the windows darkened. Jack had watched for signs of life for a few weeks before giving up on the woman across the street. Jack had no great love for her apartment, but now as she looked at it she feared she might not see it again and the fear almost consumed her.

Who was she trying to kid? She was no action hero. Sure, she could break into corporate networks and personal systems, but that was entirely differently than going to some other city, sneaking down alleys and darkened doorways to confront some band of rogue crackers. She was a desk monkey for god's sake! She squinted when she saw an unshaded light bulb. She essentially lived entirely online — she didn't even know what her best friend looked like and until this moment she hadn't even thought that this was strange. She wasn't equipped to be fighting weirdoes with brainwashing programs. She couldn't possibly succeed.

Aw, fuck it, she thought and turned and walked out of the apartment and headed to the train stop.

NINE

IT WAS A ninety minute train ride and Jack was having trouble filling the time. Her nerves were jangling and every few minutes she would decide to catch a return train as soon as they stopped. But, deep down, she knew that she'd end up following through with her plan. She had gone too far to stop now. And when she thought about it, this was the most exhilarating experience she'd had since she decided to play on the right side of the rules. Hell, she had never really been much of a cracker anyway; she was always more interested in how things worked than causing problems. Her break and enter career was entirely motivated by a need to see what was on the other side and she was very good at making sure she wouldn't be caught. This was probably the most exciting thing she had ever done in her entire life. There was no way she was going to wimp out now.

She fired up her system and logged in under her old handle. She hopped onto the boards where she had originally found the information about the group she was following. According to the posting, she was currently on her way to a sort of open house for the local chapter of the Red. It was fairly well advertised among the underground anarchicracker scene, so Jack guessed that it was probably a pretty low level bunch — the kind who might stage a reenactment of the first wetware upgrade outside a high end salon. She didn't really believe that anyone at this event would be part of the sick experiment that Jack was convinced had destroyed Estella Rowan and the man in the streeters alley. But it was a start, an entrance into this underworld that Jack now felt compelled to destroy.

Now that she had decided that she was going through with it, damn the consequences, she felt a wave of calm come over her. If she believed in such things, she may have felt that she was destined for this, but Jack was not one of the handful of people who clung to the ancient ideas of a single life having a special meaning. She knew that life was random, both the events of a life and the existence of it. She knew that it didn't matter to the universe if anyone lived or died. But it mattered to her and she felt herself warming to this new role she was taking on.

She lurked on the boards for a good fifteen or twenty minutes before asking a few questions about today's event. She got decent directions from the central train station and was told to ping a certain address when she reached a particular intersection. She logged out of the board and checked the time. She still had about half an hour before the train would arrive at its stop, so she brought up her museum interface and walked over to the main desk. She took a piece of stationery and began a message.

Adrian,

I've found some information about those things we were discussing earlier. I'm doing a little digging, but it's going to take awhile before I know for sure if I'm on the right track. I'll probably be out of touch until late tonight, but I'll talk to you tomorrow.

Just wanted to keep you posted.

J

Jack sent the message and refocussed on her physical surroundings. This train was more comfortably appointed than the intraurban lines she was accustomed to traveling on, but it wasn't quite comfortable enough to accommodate the hour and a half long trip. Jack felt some annoying numbness in her ass, which she hadn't noticed when she was online, but was now starting to make her feel restless. She shifted in her seat, trying not to jostle the people on either side of her. They were both still entirely online, though, judging from the vacant looks on their faces.

Jack was now starting to become unnerved by that look, the "here in body but not in mind" stare. She remembered from her history classes in school that when the first implants were being done, many people were opposed to the whole concept. A lot of the arguments seemed completely ridiculous to Jack, as they now did to everyone who had grown up implanted at a young age. Looking around her now, though, Jack could imagine that for people who had never directly experienced the network, seeing this look on others would have been argument enough that the implants were a bad idea. She shook her head and shook these ideas out of her mind. There was a world of difference between reading messages, doing some work or playing a game while stuck on the train and the brainlessness that was the man in the street-ers alley.

The train began its negative acceleration and most of the other passengers began to refocus to their surroundings. People began to shift, collect bags from beneath their seats and talk out loud to their traveling companions. Jack slung her small bag over her shoulders and cracked her neck. She got up and headed for the door, waiting there as the train stopped. Once the train had stopped moving, a chime sounded and the door dissolved. Jack stepped into the station and immediately noticed that the air here smelled different. Jack had never physically left the city in which she had been born — physically traveling was not that big a deal when you could go anywhere in seconds just by closing your eyes and paging around a little.

She never realized that things like the smell of the air or the way the roads curved would be any different anywhere else. For a moment she was frozen by the strangeness of this train station, its layout similar but different from the one she had at home. Then she got a hold of herself and realized that the physical world was still there, was still full of all those things that make places unique and her mood went from fear and confusion to happiness that there were still aspects of life that were natural and unexpected.

She made her way through the station and out to the local train stop. She called up the directions she had been given and, as suggested, got on a train going to Northwinds. She was one of only a few other riders on this line, so was able to get a seat to herself. She looked out the windows as the train silently hovered above its magnetic track through the city. At a cursory glance, a person would be hard pressed to tell the difference between this place and Jack's home. Both cities were full of almost identical-looking tall buildings that housed apartments that were likely very similar to Jack's own room. In the city centre were even taller buildings owned by the firms.

Every city had its ten or twenty firms, each firm having centres in up to fifteen cities worldwide. The companies agreed to certain terms, including providing law enforcement and funding minor civic upkeep like the pavement. The trains were run independently by a couple of firms, as were the utilities, schools and upgrade salons. But the most important utility, everywherenet, was controlled by a cartel of representatives of all the firms. Since they all needed it, none of the firms were willing to give up ownership to another, so they had to actually work together to keep it running, strong and free.

It was raining and the light from inside the train shone on the drops that collected on the drab scene outside the train. It made the view look almost pretty, but Jack knew that in any city the most beautiful things were the bodies and faces of the fashionable people and the logos on the buildings' doors. It was no wonder everyone spent most of their time on the nets, in games, on the boards, interacting with other people they would never see in the flesh. Flesh that was mostly just a medium for enhancing a person's ability to interact on the nets, a conduit for implants, interfaces and inputs.

Jack snapped out of her philosophical reverie and consulted her set of directions. Good thing, too, since her stop was coming up. She stepped to the door and, when it dissolved, she walked forward and turned left onto the street. The train slithered away and Jack started walking toward her destination. It was still early in the afternoon, but the sun was not very strong here and it seemed dark even though there was more than enough visibility. The rain was still coming down, though lightly now and as Jack walked along the street she wished she had paid the extra fee to bring her scooter on the train.

She had the directions up and visible, as well as a connection to the underground boards. She was absently watching the conversations while checking the street signs as they flashed on as she approached the intersections. She reached the corner of Fifth and Summerdale and dutifully pinged the address she had been given. Immediately she received a download of a map to the event. She put the map up in her vision and kept walking onward.

As she neared the street where the event was taking place, she

saw the board she had been monitoring flicker and then all conversations stopped, some in mid-thought. Jack had never seen that before
and she stopped, too. She brought the board up in full focus and
tried to comment. Nothing. She paged to another board, which
wouldn't even come up at all. She tried to bring up one of the other
nets and nothing happened there either. She pinged the address she
had been given and waited. Waited. She had never waited for the
answer to a ping. Finally after what seemed like an eternity she got
back an error message she had never encountered before.

"No route to host. Please check network connection."

What the fuck is this? Jack had a bad feeling. She thought she
knew what this meant, but that was impossible. She tried connecting
again. Nothing. She brought up her emergency beacon, took a deep
breath and sent it out. She sent a message to every connected device
within five kilometres indicating that she had an emergency. Everyone in the vicinity should be looking to see what was going on, out
of curiosity or annoyance at the interruption at the very least. But
there was nothing. She checked her logs and saw that the beacon was
not sent. She was offline. Really offline, though, not just taking a
break. There was no network.

She felt herself beginning to panic and forced her breathing to
slow down. She stood stock still and tried to make sense of this. She
pulled up Network Monitor, a program that showed the strength of
everywherenet. People who worked underground or in remote loca-
tions used it to make sure there was enough strength for high bandwidth transfers, but no one needed that sort of thing in a city. At
least, Jack had never heard of anyone needing it before.

She kept her focus on the monitor and started walking back-
wards very slowly. She saw a slow rise in the graph until it was at a
constant high level. She had moved back about a metre. She quickly
pinged a well known host and had no trouble. She brought up the
monitor again and started walking slowly forward. She watched in
dismay as the network connection decreased until it was gone completely. She kept walking and it stayed down. She crossed the street
laterally and saw the network spike up again, but as soon as she returned to the other side, it flatlined back down.

She brought up the map next to the monitor and continued
along its path. Still no network. She was starting to think that the
coincidence was too unlikely and wondered what she was getting

herself in to. She had come too far to turn back, but without the backup of the nets, she wasn't sure that she had the courage to continue. She closed her eyes, turned off the visuals and opened them again. She saw the street, uncovered by the ubiquitous information in her vision. She saw the cracks in the sidewalk, the discolouration of the metal in the walls. She looked up and saw the infinite varieties of grey making up the colour of the sky. She blinked a few times, took a deep breath and kept on moving.

She had studied the map enough that she could almost still see it before her, even though her visuals were off. She knew that the door she wanted was one block up, on the left. A red door, with the number 17 above the transom. She heard music pulsing as she approached the area and knew the door even before she saw its colour and number. She steeled her nerves, walked up to the door and pushed.

TEN

JACK FOUND HERSELF in a small vestibule before a locked metal grating at the bottom of a long, narrow, straight stairwell. A voice crackled from a speaker in the ceiling.

"There's network here. Upload the map you were given so we can confirm the checksum."

Jack drew a deep breath and turned her system on. She was, indeed, online, though the signal was weak. She found that an address had been sent to her and she replied with a copy of the map. The upload seemed to take forever, but almost immediately as soon as it was done a buzzer sounded and the grating in front of her swung open. Jack walked up the stairs, jumping as the grate behind her clanged shut. She checked the monitor to discover the already weak signal getting weaker with each step she took. By the time she reached the top of the staircase, she was offline again.

She turned left at the top of the stairs and was first greeted by a large image showing herself from a few minutes ago when she was standing at the bottom of the stairs. The quality of the imagery couldn't touch what she got from her micro recorders but its graininess only served to make the situation more unnerving. Jack looked around and noticed the recorder near the speaker. The image on the viewer jumped to show the now empty stairwell.

Jack walked into the main entrance and saw a room to her left with a few people milling around several viewers and whole lot of cables. On her right was a table with snacks and drinks, a couple of people sitting behind the table talking to the guests and a couple of

viewers behind them. Jack moved to the room to her right and noticed that the viewers in this room were showing images of the goings on in the other room.

She walked up to the table and took a beer. She wasn't taking any
chances and made sure it was unopened. "Hi," she said to the two
people behind the table, "I'm boxenjester." She gave the identity she
had been using on the outlaw boards. It felt strange to say the word
aloud; it had been many years since she had said that name.

"Nice to meet you," the man on the left said. "They call me mojo
and this is lafayette," he said, turning to the woman on his right.
lafayette smiled and said, "The stuff is all free," pointing to the
drinks and snacks, "but we'll be taking donations for the work later
on." She grinned disarmingly and Jack smiled back.

"But, uh," Jack said, not wanting to seem stupid, but legitimately
unsure, "how?"

The two at the table laughed and mojo said to the woman next
to him, "We really ought to put up signs or something at these
events."

lafayette nodded and turned to Jack saying, "You know how you
uploaded the map in the stairwell?" Jack nodded. "Well, we have
nodes that can create a localized wireless access point to our network. We'll turn one on when it's time to hit everyone up for
money." She winked and Jack found herself smiling in spite of herself.
The pair seemed friendly enough and Jack knew that they almost
certainly were not the people responsible for Estella Rowan and the
man from streeters' alley. But, she needed to remain focussed on why
she was here. It wasn't to meet new and interesting people. It was to
find her way to the people who were responsible for that atrocity.

Still, she knew that if she was going to get any information from
this event, she had to get along with the group here. She grinned at
the duo and said, "I guess that's pretty obvious now that I think of it.
So, where's a good place to start?"

"We've got examples of some of our more recent actions hanging
in the gallery," mojo said and gestured with a flick of his head, "that's
the next room."

"And later we'll be screening some work from other chapters,"
lafayette added, "and talking a little bit about the philosophy of the
group. It's always great to see new people interested in our work."
She sounded genuinely interested in sharing her vision, whatever

that might be. Jack thanked them, helped herself to a beer and suggested that they might talk later. She moved on as a couple of new arrivals took her place at the table.

She sipped her beer and wandered around the room she was in. It appeared to be a working space for the group, some kind of art studio or machine shop. There were piles of random electronics, the kind you would find on a streeter's sidewalk rug and cables snaked over the floor, up the walls and through the ceiling. There was what appeared to be a half-built drone, though it did not seem to have any disk or silicon built in yet. Perhaps it was supposed to be a statue. Jack was having a hard time deciding if the group thought of itself as a low-tech engineering cult or an artistic collective.

She made her way down the only corridor in the place and found her way to the washroom. She sat on the toilet, put her head in her hands and tried to figure out what she was doing there. After a moment or two, she used the facilities, ran some cool water over her face and returned to the main room. Along her way she noticed blankets, pillows and stacks of dishes in discrete piles in that back area of the studio. She couldn't tell for sure how many people must be living there, but it was more than two or three. As she moved into the main room, she wondered what that was like, living off-network and in such close quarters with other people.

By now a few more guests had joined the gathering and were milling around the room. She was going to have to interact with the others at some point but she wasn't sure how to strike up a conversation with the other people in attendance. A very pretty androgynous looking person in a glowing green overcoat solved that problem by clutching at Jack's sleeve and gushing, "It's such interesting work, don't you think?"

Jack answered that it was and asked her new friend what was it about the work that was most fascinating. "Oh, for me it has to be the interplay between the complexity of technology and the simplicity of the performance," the critic said, clutching Jack's sleeve more desperately, "what is it for you?"

"I, uh, I'm not as... familiar with the work," Jack fumbled, "I really only heard about the group recently from a friend who suggested it might be something I would enjoy."

"Really?" Jack's companion said, leaning in toward her. Jack could smell a light dusting of perfume that she was sure was laced with pheromones coming from beneath the overcoat. Jack would have to watch herself around someone so obviously into attraction. "Oh, you'll love the work. Let me show you the gallery."

"Thank you" Jack said, deftly removing the hand from her sleeve. "I'm called boxenjester."

"Oh, silly me," her guide said, "call me Phoenix." It came out as if the word had extra syllables somehow, the breath expelled directly toward Jack's ear. She was being played and she knew it. Still, a source of information was a source of information. And Phoenix was terribly attractive, even if it was disturbingly obvious that the attraction was a creation of a clever salon. Jack let Phoenix guide her into the other room, the "gallery".

There were more people in here, talking and looking at the exhibits. There were several viewers showing examples of "the work" as well as still images framed on the walls and hanging from the high ceiling. Behind the exhibits, the walls had been painted in several colours with slogans and tags, the painting happening over time and in layers. Every square millimetre of wall had been graffitied several times over. It made an interesting and appropriate backdrop to the work on display.

"This is one of my absolute favourites," Phoenix breathily said, steering Jack to a still image on the wall. It showed several members of what Jack assumed was a Red chapter, half of them wearing gear that entirely covered their heads, made of goggles, cables and microphones, the other half looking like normal members of the public. The normal looking ones wore shirts reading BEFORE, the mechanized people wore shirts reading AFTER. They were all arranged outside a prominent upgrade salon, smiling for the image as if they were in some firm's news story.

"It was one of the first pieces," Phoenix explained, "and the salon tried to arrest the group. Of course, they couldn't pay any fine at all, so they had nothing to lose," Phoenix laughed, the sound like a feather up and down Jack's spine. "But they didn't get anywhere anyway. Artistic expression still counts for something, god damn it." Jack smiled, recognizing a common political discussion on some of the boards — where does art fit into modern society, what business value does it bring and who pays for it? Jack usually stayed away from such obvious political discussion, but she suspected that this type of question was at the core of this group's work.

"I know," she vaguely agreed. "That's some piece." Phoenix smiled and led Jack to the next installation. This was an action piece on a viewer and Jack took the seat Phoenix found for the two of them. Phoenix's right hand strayed over to Jack's left knee and stayed where it landed. Jack let it be for the time being.

The viewer showed a group of Reds slowly walking down a busy city street. They were conspicuously observing everything they encountered — buildings, signs, the pavement, other people. Some stopped to read graffiti or talk to a streeter, others simply watched everything they passed with a passive curiosity. Of course, almost all the other people were in the half daze of keeping one eye on the physical world and one eye on the nets. Even Jack noticed how the installation made it clear that the "normal" people were the ones who looked odd, as if they were automatons. Maybe it was just her recent experience with being unconnected that made her see it this way, or maybe she was just spending too much time with these people and their strange ideas. But there was no doubt who looked like the freaks.

"That's quite powerful," she said, her breathing getting a little shallow. She had a sip of her beer and inhaled deeply.

"Their work is amazing," Phoenix said. "There's nothing like it."

"I would imagine not," Jack said, "I've certainly never seen anything like it." She felt Phoenix's hand move up her leg, the heat of flesh through the fabric of her pants. She felt herself getting flush and felt a rush of heat between her legs. Christ, she thought, as if I need this now. She lightly brushed Phoenix's hand away and stood up. "I'm going to grab another beer," she said, smiling broadly, "want one?"

Phoenix looked slightly put out, but smiled back. "Sure." Jack escaped to the other room, allowing her heart rate to slow and the blood flow to return to her brain. She picked out a couple of bottles and smiled at mojo and lafayette, who were still on door duty. "I'm really impressed, so far," she said. "Those performances are incredible."

"Thanks," mojo said, seeming to be genuinely pleased by the compliment. "I like to think that our chapter has some of the most artistic members." He leaned in close and Jack could tell that he had had a few more drinks than she had by this point. "To tell the truth, some of those other chapters take the politics way more seriously than they should. I mean, the ideas are good, but it's really about the art, right?"

lafayette smiled. "Well, we think so," she said to mojo. To Jack she said, "The leaders are going to be making a presentation in about..." she looked at a stand alone clock, "forty minute or so; you'll get to hear plenty about the politics then." Jack smiled, her heart pounding. This was what she wanted — leaders, politics, a manifesto of some sort. She felt like she was getting close to something.

She also felt warmth behind her as the smell of Phoenix's cologne tickled her nose. "There you are," Phoenix said, taking the unopened beer out of Jack's hand. "I was wondering where you ran off to." mojo and lafayette smirked at each other and lafayette leaned over to Jack.

"You've got some time before anything interesting happens," she whispered, "and there's some space back by the washroom." She winked and Jack felt herself get flushed.

"Uh, thanks, I guess," she said, as Phoenix took her hand and led her toward the back hallway.

• • •

Jack found herself in the back room with Phoenix, the beer bottles safely on the floor in a corner. She had been full of tension for the past three days and had contemplated something like this only a day earlier. But here she was, in the den of the enemy, with a complete stranger... Oh, for god's sake, she thought, it's not like all the people I could fuck on the nets aren't strangers, too. She gave in and found herself enveloped by Phoenix's soft, strong arms.

Their lips touched and Jack was reminded how much more powerful body touching was to net sex. Jack hadn't been with someone physically in almost twenty years and she nearly lost herself in the sensuality of the kiss. The smell of Phoenix's hair, the feeling of it between Jack's fingers, while their mouths found each other, their tongues touching lightly at first, then more forcefully.

Jack's hand, almost as if it had its own will, crept into Phoenix's overcoat, finding the delta between the legs. "Ah," Phoenix sighed.

"Aha," Jack said, "so that's what you've got." She grinned, then the smile turned to a gasp as Jack felt those long slender fingers on her stomach, then moving slowly into her trousers and between her legs. Those fingers have definitely been enhanced, Jack thought for a brief moment, but then she she really wasn't able to think at all. They touched each other, slowly at first, then their hands moved more feverishly, working into a rhythm all their own. They kissed and grabbed each other until they both came, Phoenix first, then Jack with a stifled yell as she buried her face into Phoenix's neck.

Afterward, they stood together, panting and glowing with exertion. "Thanks," Phoenix said. "You've very nice and that was very, very nice indeed."

"Thanks, yourself," Jack laughed, the tension finally gone from her mind and body. "You'll still show me around the gallery?"

Phoenix playfully slapped Jack's cheek. "I'm not that kind, my dear. I'm genuinely interested in talking to anyone who will put up with my long winded ramblings." Jack laughed and straightened her clothes while Phoenix did the same. "Shall we go hear what the exalted leaders have to say?"

"Yes," Jack said, picking up their beers from where she'd left them, "let's."

ELEVEN

JACK FELT AS if her mind was truly clear for the first time since this ordeal began, though she was not sure that sneaking off for a quickie was the best decision she had made in the past few days. However, what was done was done and she sat with Phoenix, talking about art and the difficulties that people who do not fit into the system of working for a firm have when trying to do their work. Jack discovered that Phoenix was gainfully employed as a writer for a prominent board devoted to performance art. One of the large firms funded the board as well as many exhibitions every year.

"I didn't know that even existed," Jack said.

"It's very uncommon," Phoenix said, "I was extremely lucky to get the position. Of course, I worked for them to begin with and was active in the community anyway. I knew who to go to and what I had to do to get it." Phoenix smiled languidly and Jack understood that there were probably not very many desires that Phoenix didn't get fulfilled.

Jack laughed and said, "Good for you. I think most of us just coast through life, letting things happen to us. It's nice to meet someone who is making things happen."

"Well, you wouldn't be here," Phoenix indicated the entire room, "if you weren't interested in making things happen." You don't know how right you are, Jack thought and sipped her beer.

"Can I ask an indelicate question?" Jack said, changing the subject.

Phoenix laughed. "I would think that delicacy would be behind us by now, wouldn't you?"

Jack smiled. "You put a lot of work into..." she ran her eyes up and down Phoenix's body, "this."

"I thought you might have noticed," Phoenix answered, almost preening slightly.

"To be blunt, why?" Jack asked, looking into Phoenix's slightly orange tinted eyes. "I mean, for so much of life the body is completely irrelevant. It's a whole lot of work for so little return."

Phoenix smiled and leaned back slightly, getting comfortable. "That depends on the kind of life you live, my dear. For most people, what you said would be true. But I live my life in such a way that I spend most of my time here, in the physical world. I come to these kinds of events for the art, of course, but much more for the people, the bodies. I love the physical and I choose to live in such a way as to get as much of it as I can."

"Fair enough," Jack said. She noticed that the lights began to dim and Phoenix's hand crept over to her knee again. Jack covered the invading hand with her own and they sat together, their hands lightly touching, as a viewer screen was lowered from the ceiling to obscure the wall at the far end of the room.

The viewer screen flickered once, twice and then the image of a man who appeared to be approaching middle age appeared on the screen. He wore his hair in a strange affectation of anachronism, it was some sort of washed out brown colour with haphazard streaks of grey concentrated at his temples. It was cropped fairly short, with two small upswept waves on top of his head. He was unshaven, but not bearded exactly, more like someone who has moved into a new apartment and forgotten to program the shaving unit in the washroom.

The most striking thing about him though, was his right eye. It was missing. He had some kind of a replacement, but there was something horribly wrong with it. Everyone had some kind of augmentation and eyes were a common choice for replacement, but completely artificial eyes usually looked pretty much like the real ones. But this was like he had just shoved a black stone in the socket. It seemed like an ominous opposite number to his real eye, a flashing blue orb that seemed to emit its own light. Of course, that could just be a clever lighting trick or an enhancement, Jack thought. Still, the overall effect was definitely startling. Even if his face hadn't been projected on to a screen that was a story high, he would have commanded attention.

"Friends," he said, his voice oddly soft. "Thank you all for coming. We are holding events simultaneously around the globe today, a celebration of our work of this last year. And it is good to see you all." The image on the viewer changed to an array of viewers, each of which showed a recorder's eye view of a room not unlike the one Jack was in. Indeed, she thought she could almost pick out the live image of their event. The view switched back to the spokesman, who Jack now though of as BlackEye.

"Many of our chapters have been very active this past year," he continued, "and have done much to further the cause." He named some areas and their projects over the past year and Jack noticed that the group who was hosting the event she was attending really was one of the more artistic of the bunch, as mojo had suggested. Some of the others were more obviously political, lacking the subtlety of the salon before and after piece, for example.

"I really don't understand some of those other groups," Phoenix said, absentmindedly groping Jack's upper thigh. "There's nothing artistic about trying to disrupt the public school network of Oceania. It's just stupid and annoying." mojo had moved into the main room now and was sitting within earshot.

"We're a pretty loose association, y'know," he slurred, "I honestly don't understand a good half of what those other groups do and I frankly wonder about them, too, sometimes." On the word 'them,' he jerked his head toward the viewer. "But they're supportive as hell and they send us parts all the time, so whatever." He took a long pull on his beer and seemed to retreat into himself a little.

Jack's focus returned to the viewer and BlackEye. He was expounding on the value of the groups' actions, then segued into talking about how the world needed to see how we all used machines without even thinking, how we accepted their roles in our lives without even recognizing where we ended and they began. "We are integrated almost at birth," he said, "machines in our bodies and our bodies in machines. But who ever thinks of the machines? Do those people in the streets, in the offices, do they ever question their machines? Do they ask themselves, when they make a decision or perform a task, 'did I do that, or did my cybernetics?' We are here to ask those questions, my friends. I encourage you to keep asking those questions, every day, every where you go."

He gave some sort of salute and most of the people in the room cheered and clapped. The viewer panned to images of other gatherings, the participants applauding, howling or waving their hands in the air. Jack turned to mojo and casually asked, "So, who is that guy?"

mojo seemed to wake with a start and took his time getting his bearings. He recovered without any major difficulty, though, and Jack suspected that he had a personal recording device on him to catch any action he missed while dozing or otherwise occupied. "He's the nominal leader of The Red," mojo said, perking up slightly. "The rumour is he started the group in Europe, after totally dropping out of life in the firms and living as a streeter for a while. There's a lot of talk that he's a total outlaw, that he stole secrets from the firm he worked for or destroyed their network or something." mojo warmed up to the role of raconteur and leaned in toward Jack and Phoenix.

"They say he took out his own eye when he was on the run because his retinal print was on file with the firm and he didn't want to be found. I think that's all a bunch of marketing bullshit myself, but there's no doubt that the guy's legitimately hard core. I met him a few times in person and he's a true believer. Like I said before, this group is all about the art, but he's all about the revolution. Hard core, man." mojo leaned back, taking a sip of beer and basking in the glow of his story. Now this was the kind of detail she was after. Whether or not the hype was true, it sounded like BlackEye was the kind of person who could be behind the human control program. And the European connection added fuel to her fire.

"Where's he based now?" Jack asked.

"Vancouver, I think," mojo said.

The pacific rim, Jack thought. This is starting to come together. Aloud, she said, "Interesting. There must be an active group there."

"Oh, yes," said mojo. "It's like home base for all of us. There's classes and meetings and all kinds of stuff going on. We all visit the headquarters when we are up there."

"I'm going to be in that neighbourhood soon, myself," Jack said, technically not lying since she had just then decided to head out there next weekend. "I wouldn't mind looking them up."

"I'll give you a map when we turn on the wireless," mojo said, "just remind me."

"Will do," Jack said and mojo left to go take care of some group business. "That reminds me," Jack said to Phoenix, who was still lightly pawing at Jack's leg, "what's up with the network here? It's not just this building; it was down part way up the block."

"It's a Dead Zone," Phoenix said, as if that explained it all.

"A Dead Zone?" Jack said, "I've never heard of that before."

Phoenix laughed, "You really are a newbie here, aren't you?" Jack flushed a little, but Phoenix just patted her knee and smiled. "There are Dead Zones all over the place, in every city. The first ones were places where the everywherenet just never made it to, but most of them now have been created by the Reds. It's part of what every group does. They dismantle the infrastructure of the everywherenet in a small area and then run hardwired access into it at the perimeter of the Dead Zone."

"What for," Jack asked, "are they just being difficult, or what?"

"I think it's partly that," Phoenix said, "but it's also so they can be connected to the network, but they're in control. They turn it on, turn it off. Most of them believe that the firms are monitoring people through the nets with more than the just the week old logs and this is a way to ensure that isn't happening to them. They have all the same access, it's just metered, buffered, rerouted and wired."

"That's so..." Jack thought for the right word, "old."

Phoenix laughed. "Well, many of them do think of themselves as anachronisms."

The lights came up and lafayette walked to the space in front of the larger viewer screen. "Okay, everyone," she addressed the crowd. "You're welcome to hang out for a while, but that's it for the formal part of the show. We're going to turn on the wireless for the next ten minutes and if you feel so inclined, we'd be happy to take any donation you'd like to leave. Thanks, everyone, for coming and if you want more information about what we do, or want to be a part of our next project, leave your contact details in the guest book. There's a dead tree book on the welcome table, but if you don't know how to write, you can beam it over when the wireless is on."

Jack felt a familiar light buzz in her head and she flicked on her display. She walked over to her cash stash and pulled out a few coins for the donation jar. She also dropped her boxenjester contact card in with the euros, figuring that keeping in touch with this group wouldn't hurt her efforts to get to see BlackEye. She heard Phoenix say, "I'll show you mine if you show me yours," and saw a contact card drop into her vision.

She passed her card over to Phoenix as well, saying, "I don't know when I'll get over here again, you know."

"I don't have to see you in the flesh, you know," Phoenix said, turning toward the exit, "it's just a preference. I'll be in touch." Phoenix winked at Jack, then disappeared down the stairwell. She took a deep breath, trying not to think about how strange this whole experience was, then turned off her display. She found mojo and lafayette and thanked them for the event and information. She reminded mojo about the Vancouver map and he dropped the file on her just before lafayette turned the wireless off.

"Thanks," Jack said, "I've got to catch a train back home."

"Have a good trip," lafayette said and Jack smiled and walked down the stairwell. The metal grate at the bottom of the stairs was either unlocked or on a motion sensor, because it opened easily at Jack's touch. When she left the building, the rain had stopped, but night had come on and the street was dark. Jack walked to the train stop without turning on her display. The silence of the street seemed to make it easier to think about what she had seen and heard.

On the train she finally turned on her systems and went online. She had a message from Adrian waiting and saw that it was getting late. She decided to wait to read Adrian's message on the intercity train and was already wondering how she was going to manage an entire week at boring Bellis when she had real work to be doing.

She watched the city go by through the images on her display. The night made the lights of the buildings both warmer and more eerie. Were the firms really trying to control people through the nets? Of course they were, but was it more than just the subtle need for a job and need for normalcy that the nets reinforced? Jack didn't know the answers, didn't know if there was an answer. She rode the train to the station in a daze.

OOIOO

I'M WALKING DOWN the street, heading for the train when it hits me like the biggest download you've ever taken. The edges of my vision start to shake and I can't turn off my display even using the hard reset behind my ear. Then the display turns into something strange, a hybrid view of some kind of desktop and the street. But the street is painted in a thousand funny colours and the desktop is all wrong — there's no pointer for the files, no window to open or close. You just reach out your hand and take the file.

Just take the file. That's right, the one in front of you. And the ones next to it, all of them, take them all and put them in the other folders. This one in your pants, that one in your jacket, the ones labeled "pocket".

Don't worry about those sounds, they don't mean anything. Just follow the trail on your desktop, follow the path back to home. And stay there.

I'll just stay there, where everything is warm and safe and nice. Where I won't remember a thing. Not a thing.

TWELVE

JACK RODE THE ninety minute train home knowing she ought to use the time to get a quick nap, but was too wired to sleep. She really wasn't sure what to think about the things she had seen and heard. She was convinced that the Red were behind the attack on Estella Rowan, but she was equally convinced that the people she met could not have been involved. Not necessarily because they were inherently good people - Jack didn't trust her judgment that much — but because it just wasn't their style. It would offend their sense of aesthetics.

In fact, after what she had seen, she was sure that the majority of the members of the Red had no idea that things like the human control experiment were going on. Such was the nature of distributed systems. What Jack still couldn't begin to fathom was why the Red would want control over a prostitute? She didn't think it was some kind of sick art project, since Rowan had disappeared and it's not art if it's not on display. But what use was she? She couldn't have been a threat to them, could she?

I've had a few lovers who've been known to be a little chattier than necessary, Jack thought and maybe one of them said too much. It could have been a tool to keep her from spilling what she'd learned. But she couldn't see why, if they were as ruthless as it seemed, they wouldn't just kill her; why destroy her mind? And what about the man in streeters alley? How did he fit in?

Jack's mind was turning in circles and she wasn't getting anywhere. She fired up her display and started paging through her messages. There were the usual daily barrage of ads, subscriptions she should have cancelled and correspondence she didn't want to deal with. Instead, she paged to a new message from Adrian and brought it up on her display.

> J.
>
> I realize you've already gone off on your wee adventure, but I feel compelled as your friend to remind you that fucking with people who turn other people's minds to mush may be hazardous to your health. I expect you to call as soon as you get this message so I can stop worrying. You'll be the death of me yet! And you used to be such a nice girl. You're too young for a mid-life crisis. Call me.
>
> A.

Jack chuckled. Adrian was cute, but Jack had to admit that her friend's half-serious warning did ring true. She should be careful, having seen first hand what these people could do. Still, she wasn't about to give up now. It was nice of Adrian to care, so Jack fired back a reply.

> Adrian,
>
> You can quit worrying, I'm alive and well. And, thanks for the warning, but I'm doing fine. I'll talk to you later with a real update.
>
> J

Jack closed the messenger and brought up her schedule. She had a full work week ahead of herself, so there was no chance of getting up to Vancouver sooner than the upcoming weekend. As much as she was anxious to get out there and confront BlackEye, she knew she could really use the next seven days to get more information and prepare herself.

She closed her scheduler and her eyes. She thought about a quick catnap, but realized that the train would be pulling into the station before she would even get into the useful part of sleep and she would just end up more tired than she was before. She opened up a tile game program and searched for players online. She found a group with whom she'd played a few times before and killed the next few minutes battling it out with them. After a mildly embarrassing loss, she thanked the other players and signed off, her mind unable to focus on the strategy.

She pulled up Phoenix's card and saw the usual message IDs as well as a link to a net location. Jack paged over and found herself in an immersive 3D video of Phoenix's art column. It wasn't live or terribly interactive, but Jack passed a few minutes paying very little attention to the content of Phoenix's talk. She set up her system to automatically grab new entries and switched offline as the train was slowing into the station.

There were fewer passengers at this time of night, so she was able to stretch out a little and work the kinks out of her neck and back. As the train stopped, she got up, making sure she had her bag with her. She hadn't needed its contents after all, but she'd felt better knowing it was there. She walked briskly to the train stop and hardly waited at all before catching the line to her neighbourhood. As the train passed a group of streeters, she was sure she saw someone with that nightmarish vacant expression she had seen on Estella Rowan and the man in streeters alley. She shook her head and hoped that she was so tired that she was just seeing things that weren't there.

She arrived in her neighbourhood and got off the train, still feeling a little shaken by the images in her mind. She passed a few streeters on the way to her building, but they were alert and aware, if not entirely benign. Jack avoided any confrontations, though, and pushed open the door to her apartment just before 0100 UTC.

Ugh, she thought, I'm going to be a wreck in the morning. She grabbed a glass of water and drank it down, then made sure the birds were set. She stripped, stuffing her clothes in the autoclave and fell into bed. She was asleep almost instantly.

• • •

Jack swore one of those fucking birds clipped her nose. She pounded on the off button and stomped into the bathroom. She showered, dried herself and sucked back a cup of coffee. Her eyes felt glued shut, but the coffee helped a little. She dressed and grabbed two breakfast bars — she was always hungrier when she hadn't had enough sleep. She was out the door and on the way to the train stop in no time, which was exactly how it felt. As if no time had passed since she was last here, getting off the train. Christ, woman, she thought to herself, waiting for the train, it's not like you're in your forties anymore. You've got to stop doing this. She admonished herself, admitting that the past few days had been more invigorating than any other time in her adult life. She boarded the train and noticed the same courier she had seen last week, looking much more chipper than she felt. She gave him a big smile anyway, though, happy for the sense of normalcy she got seeing familiar faces. He shyly smiled back, then disappeared off the train at an early stop.

By the time Jack made it to her cube at Bellis she was feeling more like an organic human being. She even remained in full control of her temper when Tony bounded over to her and thrust his foot at her. He was wearing some sort of hideous white laced shoes with some kind of a floppy thing poking out the top of the laces, on which was stencilled some foreign looking word. "Aren't they to die for?" Tony squealed, nearly falling over from bouncing on one foot.

"Well, I do think of death when I see them," Jack muttered. Tony was clearly not listening.

"They're 100% authentic genuine replicas," he sighed. "The best thing ever." His gaze caught someone else arriving and he practically flew to the door to share his joy.

Takes all kinds, Jack thought, heading over to her cubicle. Gilles was still on weekend, so Jack had no specific report to look over, though she had access to them all if she was looking for reading material. She started her beginning of the work week routine and opened the consolidated logs for the past few days, just checking up on everything. There was nothing that jumped out at her, but her mind wasn't really on it. She had determined that Bellis didn't have anything to do with the events of the past week, that they were just a random stop along the way between the Red and Estella Rowan's poor destroyed mind.

Jack scanned the usual glut of messages that accrued after a few days off. Most of them were Bellis propaganda that she ditched unread, but there were a couple of real messages hidden amongst the crap. First, she opened a note from Mac, the Eastern system guy, thanking her for her help and pointing out that all was well again. She wasn't about to clue him into the falsity of that notion, just hit the ACK button and moved on. The other message was from Gilles, saying that he hoped all was well and they he'd see her the next day. She hit acknowledge immediately, knowing that the message was a coded way of asking if she was all right. Aw, she thought, I never knew he cared.

She started on her report for the day, keeping it light and frothy, letting Gilles know that she was fine. She also started putting together an encrypted personal file cataloguing the information she knew and hunches she had formed. She figured that she would probably need to fill in both Adrian and Gilles before she left for Vancouver and she had better start getting all the information organized.

She made sure that she was signed into the underground boards under her boxenjester name, mostly just to keep maintaining a presence there. She also ran a scraper to archive all the posts so she could scour through them later for any useful information about the Reds and BlackEye.

Technically, you weren't supposed be using your own system when you were on the clock, let alone working on personal projects, but Jack had never really taken that, or any other, policy seriously. She ran a blocker that made it look like she was only running the Bellis system and was a master at watching multiple displays simultaneously. Jack figured that one of the perks of working security was being able to choose which rules you obeyed.

She spent the day alternately poking at the Bellis logs, reading and posting to the underground boards and preparing her two reports. She stayed in her cube most of the day, getting up just briefly to heat up a lunch pack from the stash in her drawer. When the end of the day rolled around, she finished off her report for Gilles and restarted her own system along with shutting down the Bellis system, the final step in ensuring her private work went unnoticed. She headed for the door, having spoken to no-one since Tony accosted her earlier.

She caught the early train and made it home in record time. She had work to do and she needed to get to bed early. There was no time to waste. She threw some food into the zapper and fired up her homemade interface. She knew that if she didn't get a hold of Adrian the universe would explode, so as she stirred her dinner she sent the request to Adrian.

She had a mouthful of something warm and edible, expecting to leave a message for Adrian to call back when the Escher flashed and the pleasant audio alert sounded, saying, "Incoming realtime secure message from... Adrian."

"Mmrf," Jack said, swallowing quickly, "okay." She focussed on her system and saw herself stride over to the Escher.

>Adrian, hi.
>>Howdy, J. Glad to hear from you.
>I know, you've been very chatty these last few days.
>>Hey, what can I say, someone has to keep an eye on you.

>(laughter) Thanks.
>>So… what's the good news?
>I learned some interesting things, but nothing concrete yet.
>>Hmfp.

Jack imagined a sound of disapproval, though she had never actually heard Adrian's voice. Apparently Adrian worked long and irregular hours and was rarely alone, so they had never had an audio or visual conversation. Jack had never thought about whether this was strange or not until now. Lately she had begun noticing how much of life was conducted over the nets, where voices and bodies were optional.

>Hey, Adrian?
>>Yeah?
>What do you look like?
>>Where the hell did that come from? And what kind of a question is that, anyway? Jesus, that's one of the joys of modern life — it doesn't matter what you look like anymore. God, Jack, you're not turning into one of those anti-net freaks, are you?
>No, sorry, I didn't mean to be offensive. It's just that all of a sudden it seemed weird that I don't have an accurate mental picture of you.
>>Sure you do. How my body looks has nothing to do with who I am, same for you. How you picture me is as real as anything else since it's based on what you know of me. When the vast majority of the people in your life are people you'll never see in the physical world, your imagination is all that matters. Come on, man, this is elementary etiquette stuff you learn as a kid.
>I know, I'm sorry. It just all of a sudden seems weird. Like if you say the same word over and over again fifty times it stops meaning anything and sounds unfamiliar.
>>…
>…
>>And you were wondering why I was worried?
>(laughter) I'm fine, really. Look, I'm working on a complete report. I'll send it to you when it's done; it will probably take a couple of days, though.
>>Days?! What have you been up to?
>It's not that much, but I'm adding stuff all the time. Besides, you'll want it thorough, right.
>>Abso-fucking-lootly.

Jack laughed.

>>Okay then, I'll wait for your little report.
>Good.
>>But you better keep in touch.

>I will, don't worry.
>>Don't worry. Ha! As if. Okay. Talk to you later.
>Later.

Adrian broke the connection and Jack shifted focus from her display to her room. Adrian's response to her non-sequitur was pretty normal; asking someone what they look like was pretty much the same as asking their weight or bank balance. Still, she found it a little odd that her friend refused to answer the question. She would have answered. Hell, she would have answered any of those questions if Adrian had asked. She thought that was what friendship was, sharing those things you don't tell just anyone. But, maybe that's not what it was. She wasn't sure that she was qualified to know the answer.

THIRTEEN

THE NEXT DAY, Jack arrived a little early, hoping to catch a few minutes with Gilles. She rounded the corner to their shared cube and smiled broadly when she saw his craggy face. "Morning, Gilles," she said, throwing her jacket on the rack.

"Hey, yourself," Gilles said. "How was your weekend?" She could have sworn that he winked at her.

"Pretty interesting," Jack said, "I'll be giving you a full written report later." He laughed and Jack smiled and lowered her voice. "No, really, I'm not kidding. There have been a lot of developments since our little adventure and I want to fill you in."

"Good," he said, packing up and getting ready to leave. "I, on the other hand," he said, "have nothing to report." He put on his jacket. "You can read all about it today," he grinned and slapped Jack on the back. "Later, dude." Jack watched him walk down the corridor and out of the office. She had been on days opposite Gilles for a few years now and they had developed a very cordial working relationship. They had their little jokes and amusements, they shared pet peeves about their fellow co-workers and made coded disparaging remarks about their bosses. They were pretty good work buddies. Jack didn't know anything about Gilles at all.

In fact, she had taken a huge risk in trusting him to help her with the break in at Buyside. She had taken the leap of faith and gone with what she knew of his personality from a couple of years of work jokes and funny reports. No one had come from Internal to arrest her, so it seemed like her hunch had been correct, but only now did she recognize what a risk it had been. And it was the same with Adrian, Adrian who didn't even feel close enough to Jack to share physical world details. And these were her closest friends, her only friends, really. It sure made a girl feel loved.

Jack logged into the Bellis system and settled into the chair, taking a few seconds luxury to feel it conform to her body. There was something almost decadent in the way the machines in the chair worked to make her comfortable. She ran the usual programs and started going through the messages and logs. She opened Gilles' report and skimmed through his usual banter about boredom, colleagues and missing lunches from the team fridge.

Jack watched one of the logs scroll up and out of her view, not really seeing it but unconsciously monitoring it for anomalies through some sixth sense or mystical power generated through years of repetitive tedium. She usually daydreamed while she worked — an occupational hazard — but this time she thought about her work, her life, the strange situations she had been in the last few days.

Almost everyone's life was pretty much like hers. Day in, day out — go to a job, do some things for most of your time that feed into a bigger complex that ultimately makes money and power for the firm. The firm then gets bigger and more powerful, making more things for people just like Jack to do every day and more things to buy and consume with their precious few days off every once in a while.

And on those days off, what do all those free people do? They play games, go shopping, have sex, watch vids, pretty much all on the nets. Most people leave one cubicle at work to go sit in another cubicle they call home. Even the nets are essentially just virtual boxes to hide in — store shaped boxes, theatre-style boxes, boxes filled with naked virtual bodies. Jack knew that the nets had the potential to offer almost limitless freedom within its confines; it wasn't real so you could do anything. But it wasn't like that.

Sure, there were pockets of rebellion and discontent, the underground boards that Jack's alter ego boxenjester frequented for example. But the freedom to talk trash about the firms was one thing, the freedom to live an entire life unbound by the laws of either physics or men, that was another thing entirely. No such freedom was to be found in the nets and Jack wondered why. She wondered how many people were satisfied with their lives, how many even questioned if this was how they wanted to live.

She snapped out of her reverie as a chime sounded. It was a message from Tony. Ugh, Jack thought, there's someone who knows what he wants out of life. All it takes is a pair of old shoes and he's happy. She answered the chime, "Talk to me."

"Hey, Jack," Tony said, "have you seen the board by the break room?"

"No," Jack answered, thinking he sounded more subdued than usual, but still leery of getting embroiled in some long conversation about waistcoats and dirndls.

"I think Atomu in finance got us," he said, "either that or we're in minor shit." He broke the connection and Jack became legitimately curious. She stood up and looked toward the break room. She could see something scrolling on the board next to the fridge and a handful of people clustered around it.

Jack wasn't a big crowd follower, but Tony's cryptic call had piqued her interest. She walked over to the break area and elbowed a path through the group. She stood before the board, reading the notice. It was one of those ubiquitous office bulletin boards, a pale organic light emitting diode screen that transmitted official notices, usually reminders to clean up after yourself and so on. It was supposedly accessible only by the designated admin, but a decent practical joker could almost certainly circumvent the crappy security on the device.

Jack was pretty confident this wasn't one of Atomu's gags, though. The sign read:

Security Alert

Various items from the sub-basement four server room have been vandalized, stolen or destroyed. There is no evidence of an outside intruder, but the logs for the time period in question have been destroyed. Please be aware that a full investigation will be launched into this incident. Anyone who has any information about this situation, or any of the parties involved, must report to their supervisor immediately.

Not bloody likely, Jack thought. Some of the people here might not be the kind of people she would choose for friends, but she didn't think any of them were likely to rat out a co-worker. Although you never knew who would be willing to be an asshole in order to curry a mote of favour with the bosses. She looked around, eyeing the others to see if any of them looked like they were about to go running to the supervisor's room with accusations.

Jack went back to her cubicle, slightly more suspicious of her co-workers than she would like to admit. She didn't really think any of them were responsible, but she was starting to fear that someone would try to pin the blame on someone else in order to get a gold star. She didn't like that — didn't like the idea of turning in your co-workers and didn't like believing that any of them would actually do that. I wish I never walked over there, she thought sulkily.

She opened her messages and poked through the deleted items area, looking for any other information about this situation. She actually read every one of them, looking for more about the server room situation. There was nothing but the usual bullshit about logos, branding and team building exercises. She paged over to the Bellis internal news page and its bright sunny graphics of unnaturally happy looking people in cubicles. She scanned through the profiles of random employees, like "Meet Sandy, the new Eastern sysadmin who likes bunnies and plays competitive Battle Ogres." She skipped past the images of last month's Birthday Club from the payroll department, a horrid mandatory five-minute affair each month with cake-style food bricks and free coffee.

She found nothing in the internal news about the incident and finally decided that as a Security Officer Class 5, it was her responsibility to find out if the sign was real or a very good hoax. She set her system to roaming and headed out of the Security room. In theory, Security staff could go anywhere in the Bellis building, still connected to the Security system. All other positions had a shutoff at the door, to prevent people from wandering too far from their desks, Jack guessed. It was like making people come in to an office in the first place — ludicrous, but effective in breaking the spirit and bending the will. Still, as a Security staffer, she could come and go as she pleased — as long as she could explain it in full detail to her supervisor.

Whatever. She decided it was her job to find out if there really was a problem in sub basement four or not. She made it into the lobby without anyone asking what she was up to, which seemed strange enough. She caught the down lift and clung to its central post as she rode the small platform down to the fourth floor below ground level. By the time she reached the ground floor, her system was being pinged by her boss. Jack answered and heard her supervisor, a man whose name she never learned, say, "So... on a little jaunt are we?"

His condescending tone always infuriated Jack and she fought to keep her voice even. "The admin sign by the security room break area may be malfunctioning. I'm checking to see if what it's reporting is real."

"I see," her boss said, obviously unaware of the sign or its message. There were enough levels of bureaucracy that it was common for the right hand to be oblivious to the left, so his lack of knowledge didn't surprise Jack. "Well... I want a full report when you have investigated. And be sharp about it. Those logs don't read themselves, you know." He broke the connection and Jack stepped off the platform and into the lobby of sub basement four.

It was dank and dark, exactly what you'd expect of a floor that was almost exclusively occupied by machines. She marched down the narrow hall toward the server room, a large locked area at the end of the corridor. The lights flickered slightly and Jack thought she could hear a slow drip off in the distance. She wondered what it was; even Bellis wasn't rich enough to let water just drip onto the floor.

As she approached the server room, she could hear the hum of the machines. It was a sound she had always found comforting, though in the dark of the sub basement she thought it sounded a little bit eerie. She heard the door unlock in response to her proximity and she pulled it open. She was unprepared for what she saw.

The machines looked like they had been gutted, as if the intruders had opened them with hatchets or crowbars. There were wires and cables everywhere, trailing over the floor and other machines, leading toward the door. The scene was strange but oddly familiar. Jack had seen something like this before, in images accompanying the story of the theft in Brugges. She turned slowly, surveying the scene. There were no cameras in the server rooms, since it was so rare that there were ever people in them that it seemed a waste of security euros. Jack sought to rectify that problem.

She systematically went through every room of machinery, on all ten sub basements, dropping micro recorders in each. She made up a cock and bull story for her boss about checking all the rooms for theft to explain why she was on the move and hustled between them all, chucking a micro recorder in the open door and moving on to the next room. By the time she was done, she had almost used all the small spheres, but that was fine. The truth was that she'd never had a good reason to buy them and this way she might actually learn something about what was going on.

Once she had recorders in every room, she caught the lift back up to her floor and marched back to her desk. The group by the break area had broken up by then but as soon as she got to her cube she found Tony streaking over. "Where have you been," he half whispered and half screeched, "did you get hauled in? What's going on?" He looked like he had worked himself into a pretty good lather about the whole situation. Jack knew he was high strung and tried to pacify him with the almost whole truth.

"Tony, man, we're Security," she said, trying to act like a cool leader from some vid. "We don't make trouble, we fix it. I was checking out the scene, seeing what we can do to figure out what happened down there."

She hoped that this would calm him down, but it seemed to get him even more worked up. "So it's real?" His voice rose in pitch and volume. "There really was an intrusion?"

"Yup," Jack said, seeing no way out of this conversation, "but it's no big deal. They took a couple of drives and wrecked up the place a little, that's all. It was probably just some pissed off clerk." Tony got ready to panic some more, then seemed to take in what Jack had said. She breathed a sigh of relief as he seemed to buy her pile of bullshit and calmed down.

"You really think so?" he asked, looking for reassurance.

"Yeah," she said, "I don't think it's anything to get worked up over. Management has to look into things, but I don't think they'll be bothering anyone else up here." Tony looked so relieved that Jack was afraid he might try and touch her or something, so she quickly said, "Just go on back to work. It'll be fine."

He smiled and said, "Okay. Yeah, it will be fine, won't it? Thanks, Jack." He walked back to his cube and Jack wondered, not for the first time, about his mental health. She spent the rest of the day checking the views from the micro recorders and finishing up the report for Gilles. She gave him a brief run down on what she had seen in the server room and alerted him to the Brugges incident by suggesting elsewhere in the report that he should check out "this interesting board I found." He should be able to put the two together, Jack thought, I just wish I could tell him about the micro recorders. Maybe I'll send him a message tonight. Jack finished the report, tidied up and logged out. As she left the security room, she saw Tony getting ready to leave also. He smiled weakly and Jack gave him the thumbs up sign. Man, he's a crazy one, she thought.

FOURTEEN

JACK SPENT THE evening going over the Brugges theft, comparing it to the incident in the Bellis server room. There was more information about the European crime by now, on the regular news boards as well as the specialized ones Jack has been paging through before. It seemed that the theft had been conducted by a pair of locals who had now gone missing. There didn't seem to be any link between the two prior to the incident; one was a service worker in a mid range upgrade salon and the other was an entertainment worker.

Rowan, Jack thought. She was an entertainment worker from Brugges. Of course, that made as much sense as anything; more, really. Most of the analysis of the event had pointed out that the logic was quite poor, but only if the thieves cared about getting caught. If you had no thoughts of you own, why would you care about the logs, getting caught or having to disappear?

Armed with this information, Jack did some more digging, trying to find any data that could prove or disprove this theory. She ran a search for Rowan's name, but came up with nothing she hadn't already seen. She scanned through the more speculative information about the Brugges theft and finally came across some blurry images enlarged from satellite views of the area. The images were of predictably bad quality and it would never be possible to identify someone from them alone. There wasn't enough of a face recognizable to run through the recognition programs to get a match, but Jack immediately saw the resemblance.

Beautiful Red

It was Estella Rowan, along with someone Jack didn't recognize, leaving the area with armloads of equipment. There was no question in Jack's mind that the image on her viewer — larger than life, albeit highly pixellated — was the same as the face she had seen when she struggled with Rowan's broken consciousness. On the other hand, the woman in the image Jack had seen when she searched through the public area of Rowan's mind was nowhere to be seen.

Jack closed the image and turned her viewer off. She sat at her table, grieving for Rowan anew. She had never known the woman, maybe wouldn't even have liked her. Hell, there was no reason to think they would have been friends, no reason to believe she was even a decent human being. Maybe she skimmed from her employer, cheated her clients, was mean to streeters. Still, Jack couldn't get past the images she had seen during her visit to Rowan's system. What must it be like to have such a conflict inside your own mind? And what had happened to her body? It seemed like the kind of fate no one should have to endure.

Jack took a deep breath, banishing the images from her mind. She couldn't help Estella Rowan any more than she could stop the earth from spinning. She could, however, track down the people doing this and expose them or stop them or something. So she set her mind back to the task at hand — getting the evidence she needed and finding out as much as she could about the Red and the man she thought of as BlackEye.

She copied all the relevant information about the Brugges heist to a local file, including the blurry image of Estella Rowan. She searched through her own cache in the hopes of finding an image of Rowan from Jack's visit to her consciousness. Jack chose to run the search in command line mode, not wanting to relive the experience by seeing the images. Jack kept a fairly large cache file as a matter of course, so she was not surprised to find the record of her experience in Rowan's mind. She added the image to her report without looking at it.

She sat up, cracked her neck and got a beer from the fridge. She realized she hadn't eaten anything and heated up a meal in the zapper. As she ate she scanned the boards for any incidents similar to what had occurred in Brugges the previous week and at Bellis the previous night. She had trouble narrowing the search down, as theft of equipment was common enough. She eventually ended up on the

IA board where she had previously read analyses of the incident. She checked for any new posts on the Brugges topic and any related information.

She scanned the posts one by one, looking for any new leads or references to other incidents. Finally she found it: a post by one of the intelligent agents linking other similar incidents. It was a hell of a resource — a list of similar events and links to more information about them. Jack followed all the links and as she paged through the evidence collected by the agent, a clearer picture began to form in her mind.

All over the globe, over the past month or so, strange thefts had been occurring. They were all brazen attempts, leaving obvious evidence of the assault. The reports were filled with images of disemboweled equipment, cables and wires in torn and tangled piles on the floor. In none of these incidents had the perpetrators bothered to hide their crime, but any security recorders or logs had been disabled or destroyed. The satellite image from Brugges was the best image of the thieves from any of the scenes.

The targets were all over the map, geographically and in terms of their natures. There were various machine rooms of large firms, warehouses of parts for a major wholesaler, the back room of an upgrade salon. The common denominator was the equipment taken. It was exclusively disk. In total, enough memory was taken to power a small firm's server room. And both Jack and the agent who had collected these examples believed that this was just the tip of the iceberg. Surely only the larger targets had gone public with these thefts and that was only because with so many employees someone was bound to leak the information. Their PR departments would be sure to put the information out first to make sure that the correct spin was on the story. Smaller outfits would cover up the damage and pretend nothing happened so as to not alarm their clients and investors.

Jack wondered about this epidemic of theft and the stolen disk. It cost a bundle to get a huge pile of memory, sure, but the effort to subvert the logs and recorders wasn't free either, not to mention the cost in human lives and minds. Jack couldn't imagine that many people would be enticed into such an act by even the amount of money it would take to buy that amount of disk retail, so it had to be some kind of coercion. Jack was convinced that the thieves were all under the same control as Rowan had been; it was the only explanation for why people would willingly put themselves at risk of arrest and have to essentially disappear after the crime.

For the next hour, she mechanically ate her food and sipped at her beer while paging through the boards. If the woman in the building across the street sat at her window and increased her vision five times, she would see Jack sitting at her table, transfixed on something a million miles away that only she could see, occasionally feeding her body. The woman across the street would turn from the window, thinking what an unremarkable life Jack led and carry on with her own evening plans.

You could look in almost any window in almost any city in the world and nine times out of ten you would see exactly the same scene. People, home from work, eating food to keep their bodies alive, while their minds and visions lived on the nets. They played games, visited with friends real and imaginary, did everything people did when they weren't at work.

• • •

Jack was deeply immersed in her research when the Escher started flashing. "Your timing sucks, Adrian," she muttered aloud as she switched over to her 3D interface. She walked toward the flashing fish and noticed that it wasn't Adrian calling after all. The connection originated from the Bellis system. It was Gilles.

> >Hey G. This is a surprise.
> >>I know you can't get enough of me.
> >(laughter) Who could?
> >>I just thought I'd give you a teaser to tide you over 'til the morning.
> >Such a kind hearted guy.
> >>So, I was reading your report and wanted to check a few things.
> >Such as?
> >>You went down there and saw it?
> >Yup.
> >>And it's like the one from Belgium?
> >Exactly.
> >>...
> >You know something I don't?
> >>I doubt it... You're looking into it now, aren't you.
> >Yup.
> >>Get anything?
> >Yup.
> >>Anything good?
> >I think so.
> >>Are you gonna share?
> >I'll put it in the report.

>>When are you planning on passing that on?
>A couple of days. Before the weekend.
>>Okay. Good.
>...
>>...
>Since when are you interested in this stuff?
>>Always was, kiddo. Since before you were born, probably.
>Christ, I keep forgetting you're older than dirt.
>>What's dirt?
>Funny stuff. See ya tomorrow, champ.
>>Later, dude.

Jack disconnected and wondered what was up with Gilles. He had helped her break into Buyside and he had sent that message while she was off at the Red party on the weekend and she was sure the conversations of the last week or so were the longest they had had in the entire time they had been working together. She knew he was as bored as she had been at work and maybe he was just finding this all to be a pleasant distraction from the ennui of work.

Maybe she was just over analyzing everything, or maybe she really was getting paranoid. She checked the time and groaned when she saw that she had less than eight hours until she had to be back at Bellis. She double checked her report and saved it to an encrypted area in her system. She stripped off her clothes and threw them in the autoclave on the way to the bathroom. She showered and sucked back a dose of SleepingJuice. She started thinking about what it might feel like to have an alien program in your mind when she fell into sleep. If she dreamed, she didn't remember it.

• • •

The next few days were nearly clones of each other: work, home, research, then sleep. During the day, Jack was keeping half an eye on the logs and Gilles' reports and the rest of her attention was focussed on researching the Red. After her shift was over, she would return to her apartment, stuff food in her face and continue her studies. She was like a brainy child with a learning compulsion, or maybe it was more like an addiction. She couldn't stop herself.

She started with the boring stuff — history and news reports. The Red had been founded about a couple of decades previously, around the time that implants were becoming common. As integrated technology became more and more standard, the Red stepped up their operations. Jack was surprised to learn that their first taste of notoriety came when a small group of people in Asia got caught with a crate of stolen implants. They had been reprogramming them and distributing them in the community.

The article Jack found implied that the thieves were claiming to be members of the Red as a justification for what the author believed to be outright theft for profit. Other members of the Red who hadn't been involved had come to their defence, though, and argued that it was a social justice operation to redistribute technology to the un- or under-employed. As she read further, Jack guessed that the author of this article got it wrong. She found reports of several examples of Red actions that were similar — refurbishing nodes salvaged from recyclatrons, leaving expensive gear in areas known to be frequented by streeters, a few other high profile thefts that mimicked that first incident.

Eventually, Jack got tired of reading the same old reports about the Red. It seemed that only a handful of their activities got a lot of coverage on the mainstream news boards and the same instances kept coming up over and over. Jack spent an hour or so scouring the boards and making clever small talk before she got a link to an internal Red board. She paged over, but as soon as she arrived at the new site she found that she wasn't able to authenticate to the board. She grinned and set to work.

It took a whole evening. The next night, though, she paged over to the Red board and could see it all: images, 2D video, 3D immersives and, of course, all the text she could hope to read. It was all one way, though; Jack had taken pains to make sure she didn't appear as a member on the board. She lurked in peace as she opened a few immersives detailing the recent projects in Paris and watched a video about a protest outside a nutrient block factory.

After she had watched a few more, Jack realized there wasn't really anything in the videos that she hadn't seen at the event the previous weekend, so she started wading through the text content. The text archives were massive and included everything from home-grown manifestos to articles on reprogramming implants to logs of chat sessions. Jack tried to focus on the policy documents, but she found herself gravitating toward the technical how-tos. After realizing that she had been reading a manual for an obsolete visual enhancer for over an hour, she refocussed on the physical world and poured another glass of water.

She downloaded the manual and several others like it, then returned to the manifestoes and screeds. Like everything else she had learned about the Red, they were diverse and varied from so moderate even Jack held more unconventional opinions to the extreme. Jack started alphabetically.

• • •

On the fourth day of her studies, she was interrupted by the program that responded to the micro recorders. She had long since given up on learning anything from them, there had been no activity since she had dropped them in the various basement rooms at Bellis. But now, all of a sudden, the small monitor began to chirp, indicating that one of the recorders had picked up some motion and begun recording and transmitting.

It's probably just some malfunction, Jack thought, even as she switched away from the nets and brought up the recorder's visual images. At first she thought that it was, indeed, a problem with the recorder, as she could see nothing but an empty warehouse. She was about to switch back to the nets when a movement off to the right caught her eye. She switched to the full immersive view and somewhat nauseously found herself seeming to stand in the middle of what looked like the equipment warehouse in the ninth sub basement.

At first everything was still, then Jack saw a slight movement at what seemed to be the door. Because of the placement of the recorder, she couldn't see the door straight on; the recorder had landed off to the side of the entrance, so she was looking into the room from just to the left of the inside of the door. She instinctively craned her neck, but of course she couldn't adjust the angle of the view no matter how she moved her body. She saw a figure enter the room, its dark silhouette framed against the faint light coming from the open doorway. It moved into the room with a slow, shambling walk, headed straight for the racks of surplus or reserve servers.

Jack held her breath, waiting to see what happened, when the door banged open and two more people lurched into the room. She had audio, but they made no sound except for a ragged breathing and the shuffling of their feet. The two newcomers followed the path of the first person in the room and the three of them approached the servers. They seemed to stand there, as if they were waiting for something or someone else to arrive. Then, all of a sudden and in unison, they began to tear open the servers with their bare hands.

Jack heard a small shriek of protest, then realized it was her own voice as she felt her body flinch from the view. The three of them were ripping open the servers, their hands and nails getting cut and torn from the metal of the cases, but even as they were clearly injuring themselves not one of them made a sound. It was as if they could not even feel their own bodies. They opened up the servers and ripped out the disk inside, stuffing the memory into the many pockets of their clothes.

At this point Jack noticed that they all wore Bellis uniforms. Thinking about it, this should have been no great surprise, as there was no way to access the sub basements other than with current security clearance, but Jack still found it shocking. Jack watched in horror as the three intruders methodically destroyed every server in the room and ripped out the disk inside. It seemed to go on forever, but in less than five minutes after they began the room was littered with cable, wires and bits of metal from the cases. They scoured the room for any dropped or missed bits of memory and in the process one of them turned toward the recorder. It was no one Jack recognized, but she got a good look and would be able to run the image through a program to identify the employee. It was a man, who as he approached dropped a piece of metal on top of the micro recorder. Jack involuntarily ducked as the piece of the case seemed to grow exponentially larger and fall on her head.

She switched the viewer off and discovered that she was sweating. "Damn it," she said aloud. The look on that man's face was exactly the same as the man in streeters alley, exactly the same as Estella Rowan's. Jack thought fast and sent a ping to Gilles to alert him to the goings on downstairs. Before she had even decided how to explain this situation to him, the ping came back with an error. There was some kind of malfunction on the receiving end. Jack frowned and tried again while running a remote diagnostic. The ping returned the same error, while she tried to log onto the Bellis system. Nada. They're fucking with the network, Jack thought, frustrated. Just like in all the other thefts. She checked the time and realized that even if she got through to Gilles, they would be long gone.

FIFTEEN

AFTER A BEER and a contraband cigarette, Jack finally got over the frustration at her inability to do anything, then spent the rest of the night finishing her report for Gilles and Adrian. She would send it out to them before she left. With these new images from Bellis, as well as the information she had been gathering, she had a fairly complete report to send them. They had both been harassing her for updates, but she was afraid that one or both of them would try to stop her from going if she told them what was going on. She knew her fears about her friends were really her own sense of personal security trying to stop her from doing something foolish, but if she could keep anyone else from voicing those thoughts she would be able to ignore the voices in her head.

As a quick break, she booked space on the TGV for herself and her scooter. She planned to drive to the complex, since she had never been to the capital of Cascadia before and figured she ought to see the sights while she was there. Sort of a working holiday, she thought. She finished off the report, filed it away in its encrypted directory and went to bed for the last time in her own room before going into the den of the enemy. She was feeling melodramatic.

The next day was Tuesday, Jack's last day at work before the weekend. She got up early and pulled her scooter out of storage where it had been locked up for at least six months. She brought it up to her room, where it nearly filled the available space. She plugged it in to the electric socket to make sure that it would be well charged by the evening and ensured that she had a couple of jugs of veg oil in the panniers as well. She stuffed a couple of changes of clothes in a bag and shoved it in the space under the seat. She left the scooter to charge as she headed to work.

When Jack got to her cube, she saw that Gilles had left already. He left her a note reminding her to send him her report, which she trashed as soon as she'd read it, even though the Bellis system retained a log of all internal messages, trashed or kept. She spent the day so preoccupied by her weekend plans that she barely paid any attention to the new reports of another theft from the sub basements. She knew that the perpetrators had bigger problems that getting caught and fired by Bellis. They were not even really human any more, Jack figured.

She ran the one decent image she had from the theft through the corporate employee records, looking for a match. She was unsurprised when the program came back with a name - Mario Keating. Jack checked the employee record and saw that he was on weekend. In her gut she knew what the answer would be, but she pinged Keating's personal system anyway. Nothing. Jack wondered if she should break in, like she had with Estella Rowan, but she was sure she didn't want to go through that again.

She sat back in her chair, took a sip of coffee and paged over to the internal news board. This time there was a piece about the thefts and how there was going to be an investigation of all staff. Jack knew that eventually her recorders would be found and that she would have to share what she knew and at that point it would be helpful for everyone if she could point to the culprit. But she also knew that the real perpetrator wasn't Mario Keating, the cafeteria worker, it was the Red's human control program.

Aw, fuck it, she thought. She didn't want to have to go through the same experience she had with Rowan's system, so she decided to go old-school. She ran a terminal emulator and started typing in commands. She tunnelled through to Keating's system and when there was no response to her ping, she finessed her way inside. She quickly found her way to the inner sanctum, Keating's mind. It was just like with Rowan; a total mess. She finally found his consciousness, or what was left of it. She grabbed scans of his brain waves and got the hell out of there. Even in strings of characters on her viewer's screen, that was some creepy shit that Jack didn't want to be part of for long.

Just as she had logged out of Keating's system and was cleaning out any traces of her visit, she heard a voice right next to hear ear say, "What's going on, Jack?" She jumped in spite of herself and focussed on the physical space around her. It was Tony, looking pale and disheveled.

"What do you mean?" Jack asked, trying to calm both of them with a matter-of-fact demeanour.

"There was another break-in," he said, "what does it mean? Are we all in trouble?"

"I think we'll be okay," Jack said, "it's probably just streeters or someone taking stuff to sell on the black market." She knew it wasn't that believable a lie, but she figured that Tony was desperate for any kind of consolation.

"But why did they come back," he whined, "why don't they just leave us alone?"

"I don't know, Tony," Jack snapped, then as she saw his face crumble, she softened her voice, "but we're safe up here. Besides, they aren't really hurting anyone. They're just after things."

Tony gasped and said, "What do you mean, just things? What else is there? What kind of security do we have if strangers can just walk in here and make off with anything they want?"

"That's not what I meant," Jack backpedalled, trying to come up with something that would allay Tony's concerns. Eventually she pulled out the big guns, the bureaucratic equivalent of the killer end move. "I just meant that it's not our job to deal with it. Management has assigned it to another department, so we should be fine."

"Oh," he said, looking relieved. "That's good, then. So we shouldn't have to worry about it, then?"

"No," Jack said, "we should be fine." He smiled at her and mopped his soggy forehead with a piece of white cloth which he stuffed back into the chest pocket of his strange jacket. He went back to his cube and Jack wondered anew if he was having some kind of malfunction. She opened up her private report for Adrian and Gilles and filled in the new details that she had learned about this most recent incident. She finished up the report about an hour before her shift ended. She spent the rest of her day doing up a quick and dirty version of the daily report she had to keep for Bellis and trying to steel herself for the next three days.

• • •

Beautiful Red

Jack's heart pounded when she thought about trying to infiltrate the Red complex in Vancouver. She had learned that the headquarters of the group wasn't another dingy room in the Dead Zone, like the studio used by mojo and lafayette's group. Rather, there was a fairly large complex where several people lived full time and many others visited. It was sort of like a tourist destination for Red members the world over. On the one hand, that gave Jack an excuse to be there. On the other hand, there were plenty of people who would expect that she had a modicum of a clue about the group.

It was strange enough to pretend to be part of group at all; most net groups were pretty straightforward, so there was no such thing as pretending to belong. If you cared enough about the subject to be there, you were part of the group. The Red seemed different to Jack. In many ways they weren't a net group at all. They had plenty of boards and doubtlessly most of the members had only ever met online, but fundamentally they were a physical world organization. Their "actions", whether you called them crimes against society or art, were physical world events. And at their core they had beliefs that made it difficult to meet solely on the nets.

Certainly the vast majority of their members were not hard core believers and there were many levels of involvement. From the digging Jack had done, she came to realize that mojo, lafayette and the others she had met were at one end of the Red spectrum — the moderate artistic end. At the other end, among the hard core of the group, were beliefs that were counter to almost every normal opinion or way of life Jack could think of.

Hard core Reds never used everywherenet; they logged into networks using a hardwired connection only. Jack wasn't sure how this was accomplished; the documents she had seen never described the process. It was one of the many things an adherent was supposed to learn in the flesh. That was another concept common among the hardliners. Doing things in the flesh. They advocated meeting in the physical world and many a Red treatise was devoted to the concept that a physical experience was more "real" and therefore more intrinsically valuable than the same experience on the nets.

If she was going to be honest with herself, Jack found the Reds to be a confusing bunch. On the one hand, they were very much like the typical anti-progress types — "the nets are bad, the physical world is good." But every Red Jack had seen had at least some augmentations and cybernetics and they used the nets as much as anyone else. She had learned enough to get a rudimentary grasp of the lingo and although she felt completely ill prepared, she knew this was as good as it was going to get before her pilgrimage to the Red complex in Vancouver.

She finished her report and tidied up her cubicle. She logged out of the Bellis system, fought the nausea from the Everlock scan and got her jacket from the coat rack. She headed out the door of the Security Room and rode the lift down to the main floor. She walked out of the Bellis building, already starting to feel her breath quicken. She rode the train back to her apartment and barely noticed any of the other passengers even though she was offline. Her mind was buzzing so much that she almost felt as if she were online playing a high bandwidth game and reconciling her finances at the same time.

Back at her apartment, she showered and changed clothes, choosing knee length dark brown pants with several pockets, a shirt with a slight green glow to it and a bulky sweater. She grabbed a couple of cold meal packets and stuck them in one of her many pockets and loaded the others with a few essentials. She added a light silver windshell to her outfit and logged into her personal system. She pulled out her private report and prepared messages for Gilles and Adrian to envelop the report. She blind copied them both, with personalized introductions, then shut down her apartment for the next three days.

She unplugged her scooter from the floor socket and stowed the cable back in its front compartment. She pushed the scooter forward and out the door of her room. Her apartment door shushed closed behind her and she double locked it using the strong encryption key most people kept for those moments when they're paranoid. She flipped on the anti-grav chip on the scooter's chassis and it hovered a few centimetres off the floor.

Anti-grav was one of those marketing terms that sounded much cooler than it really was, since all the chips did was interact with the magnetism of the floor in such a way as to repel the object to which it was attached. Jack always found it funny when people tried to use anti-grav in places that weren't metallic. So few people bothered to find out how anything worked; they seemed to prefer to believe that everything was too complicated to possibly understand.

Now that the scooter was hovering over the floor, it was much easier to manhandle down the stairs of her building and on to the street. When she reached the street, the scooter thumped to the ground and she turned off the now-useless chip. Jack straddled the machine and brought up the control program. She sent her password to the machine and it started with a dull whir. She checked the charge and confirmed that the machine was fully powered. She also checked the bio-diesel tanks and saw that the tanks were full to about half capacity, so she figured that without topping up she could probably go for 200 kilometres on oil alone if she had to.

She checked the street for traffic, but it was quiet as usual. She pulled onto the street, accelerating smoothly. She had a live map of the area up on her left eye, while she kept the other eye clear to watch for traffic and pedestrians. It was only a few clicks to the TGV station, so the ride didn't take very long. About halfway to the station, her system gave her an audio notification that her message to Adrian had been acknowledged. Good, she thought, if something happens to me, at least I know that there's someone else who knows what I know.

She pulled into the station with a good quarter of an hour to spare. She queued up for the parking zone and was surprised to see so many other scooters, 'cycles and hover boards. Most people were happy to take the trains which could get you anywhere in a city. Of course, the capital was a gateway to many places that didn't have such a good transport system — the hinterland of the north was a popular tourist attraction among the physical world adventure types.

The parking line moved quickly enough and soon Jack was slotting her scooter into a space barely big enough to accommodate it and the panniers she had attached. She flipped on the anti-grav and hoisted the scooter up to the clamps on the side of the parking car. She slipped the wheels into the clamps and turned the anti-grav chip off as the clamps closed over the wheels, locking her scooter in place. She took an image of the location of her spot for future reference, then made her way into the passenger compartment.

She found an empty seat and settled in. The TGV ran at just over 400 km/h, so Jack anticipated that the trip would take roughly four hours. She had exhausted her capacity for research and preparation by this point, so she pulled out a meal packet and opened it just as the train was starting off. After she was done her dinner, she pulled out a bottle from one of her pockets, a three hour draught of SleepingJuice. She drank it down in one, thinking that it wouldn't hurt to sleep through this one train ride. She leaned back slightly in the chair and the dark curtain of sleep fell over her almost immediately.

OOIOI

THIS HAS TO stop. The last time I came out of a blackout, I knew that this isn't just some malfunction with the hardware, this is a real problem. I came to in my room, at my table, as I have so often in the last few weeks. I was cold, as I usually am after one of these episodes. But this time my hands... my hands were all scraped, scratched and bleeding, like I had been fighting or tearing into a bolt of glass cloth without gloves. And I have no memory of any of it.

Of course, I listened to my recordings. I listened to them over and over until I finally couldn't stand it anymore. Because there's nothing, not even background noise or hiss. The entire section of my blackout has been erased. And the log says I'm the one who erased it.

SIXTEEN

JACK WOKE UP with a start and for a moment didn't know where she was. The motion of the train was so even that it was as if the train were still. The seats were fairly wide and comfortable, so she wasn't even being jostled by other passengers. Her confusion was fleeting, though, and she checked the time. SleepingJuice was amazing — at that point the train would be arriving in about fifteen or twenty minutes.

She stretched as best she could while staying seated and cracked her neck. She quickly checked her system and found an acknowledgment from Gilles for her report. Good, she thought, at least if they turn me into one of those drooling monsters they'll both know who to blame. Jack had given both Adrian and Gilles encoded links to contact each other in case of emergency. She allowed them to talk to each other anonymously; she had no interested in dragging them into this any more than was necessary.

Jack looked out the window and saw the coastline blurring off in the distance. She drank out of the complimentary bottle of water she got with her train ticket and finished it off in one draught. She pulled up the information on her system about how to get to the Red complex. The train station was near the city centre, but the complex was out on the western-most reaches of the city. The map of the city seemed complete and she had good directions for the lay of the land at the complex. She was as prepared as she could be, so there was nothing for it but to just get going.

She felt the train begin to slow and she made sure she had all of her things. She had left most of her gear locked in her scooter in the parking car, but from force of habit she patted her pockets making sure that all the items she had stowed there were where she had left them. After her little ritual was done, she stood and leaned against the force of momentum as the train was slowing. She made her way toward the parking car, bringing up the image of where she parked her scooter.

She weaved between the rows of vehicles, guided by the image on her display. She found her scooter with no problems and hung on to it for balance as the train stopped. A notice popped into her vision advising her to activate the anti-grav chip, which she did. In a few second the clamps sprang open and she pulled her scooter down off the wall and turned it to face the exit. She turned the chip off and felt a satisfying thump as the scooter obeyed both Newton's first law and his most famous discovery.

She straddled the seat, sent her password and started up the engine. She had been able to recharge the batteries on the trip so she still had a full charge now. The big door at the end of the car opened and the line of traffic slowly filed out of the train. Jack was antsy and wanted to get moving, but there's nowhere to go when you are in a queue of traffic. Finally she escaped the train and the station and found herself on the city streets.

There was more traffic than she was accustomed to, but her map had prepared her for the traffic and the street. She took a right, deciding to take the longer but more scenic route along the waterfront. She accelerated and soon was zipping along the coastline, headed for the Red complex.

It had been some time since Jack had driven and she had almost forgotten why she had put up with the inconvenience and expense of storing the scooter. The touch of the wind through her hair, the feeling of the road rushing beneath her and the sheer thrill of moving with her machine, separate but united, were among the most pleasurable things she ever experienced. It had been too long. Some people were just born to drive, she thought and she was one of those. She pushed her scooter to the limit its electric engine would allow and on a particularly open stretch of road, flipped over to hybrid mode.

At first the engine was sluggish, adjusting to the new fuel source, but then she felt the gears change and the engine seemed to roar with life. The faint smell of real food cooking that came with the increased speed always made the experience more fun for Jack. She switched back to pure electric when the traffic increased as she neared the complex. She crossed its legal border a full five minutes before she saw the first evidence of it being the right location.

She drove up to a large building that she believed was the semi-public centre. She parked her scooter in the lot behind it, surprised that there was so much open parking space. She locked up her scooter, taking the panniers with her. She checked her system and was unsurprised to discover that she was offline. She walked back around to the front of the building and up the main steps. The large centre doors opened for her and she found herself in what seemed more like the lobby of a nice hotel than the lair of criminal crackers.

She approached the main counter, took a deep breath and introduced herself. "Hi," she said to the bored-looking man working the front desk, "I'm boxenjester and I've come to stay and learn." He didn't respond, he just looked like he was waiting for something. "I have a map," Jack said, trying to sound like a regular hopeful acolyte as she explained that mojo had given it to her and suggested she come to the headquarters to learn more.

"Fine," the clerk sighed, "send it to me." He asked if she had wireless and she frowned, since everyone did, but said yes. He flipped a switch on the desk and Jack's system came back online. She found the map and sent a copy to the clerk. The network went down as soon as the transfer was complete and Jack waited while he ran the checksum. The map must have seemed authentic enough, because he said, "Fine," again and turned his back. When he turned around again, he handed Jack a small plastic device with a prong at one end. "I've put you in room 10734; you'll find your way using that map over there." He pointed at a large freestanding board in the lobby covered in a complicated map. "Just stick the key in and it will tell you how to get there."

"Thanks," Jack said, trying for the right combination of blase understanding and gung-ho excitement.

"The next orientation session is in about an hour. Your room will tell you more." He turned away from her, obviously ending the conversation. Jack walked over to the map and after a moment to figure the system out, stuck the prong end of her device into the slot in the board. A route lit up on the map and a flashing light designated her room. It was about 250 metres away, off on the left of the central building in which she stood, on the seventh floor. She took an image of the map to her local system and yanked the plastic device out of the board. She walked out of the lobby in search of her room.

She walked down the path that led from the main building to a cluster of short, residential type buildings. She found Building Ten and entered its dingy lobby. There was not much to it, just a small space where you could wait for a lift. Jack did just that and as one of the platforms came around, she stepped aboard it and rode up to the seventh floor. She stepped off into an equally dingy hallway of concrete and metal and walked down the hall to room 34. She found the door, a solid slab of metal and stuck the prong of her key into a slot just next to the door. A small red light came on above the slot and the door slid open.

Jack entered the room and was surprised to discover that it was much the same as her own apartment. It was only slightly smaller, missing the kitchen area and the fixtures were a little less up to date, but otherwise it was very similar. Jesus, Jack thought, I wonder how much this little weekend is going to cost me? She dropped her panniers on the bed and looked around. The striking difference between this room and her apartment, or any other room she had stayed in, was the large panel on one wall. She walked up to it and saw that it looked like a viewer, a smaller version of the one at the Red party she had been to the previous weekend.

Jack wasn't sure what to make of it, but she noticed one of those now familiar slots next to the screen. She shoved the key into it and jumped slightly as the viewer lighted up and some kind of startup chime sounded. A pleasant-sounding voice came from the screen and said, "Hello, boxenjester. I am Red Five, the personal assistant for all newcomers. I am here to answer your questions, keep your schedule and help you navigate the compound and the program. The next orientation session will be held in the common room on level two in 46 minutes. I will remind again you 36 minutes from now. Would you like to see a map to the common room?"

Jack felt stupid, but said, "Yes" aloud to the bright rectangle on the wall. Immediately a floor plan of the building appeared in the rectangle, showing a large space at the far end of the second floor. "Do you have any questions?" the voice asked.

"Not yet," Jack answered, turning away from the wall viewer. She spent the next half hour sitting on the bed with her eyes closed, going through her local system. She was hoping to record much of the events of the next few days, but she knew she wouldn't have enough on-board memory to keep it all. First, she set her recording rate to the lowest settings possible to conserve space, then set up a code she could think to start and stop recording. She kept the recording program going in the background and set it to "remember". This meant that it would record constantly, but delete everything older than two minutes unless Jack thought her record code. That way, even if she was a little slow, she should be able to get everything she wanted.

She was finalizing the settings on the recorder when the Red Five voice said, "You have ten minutes until the orientation starts, boxenjester." Jack opened her eyes and looked through the cabinets near the bed. She found a case of bottled water, grabbed a bottle and drank half. She stoppered the bottle and slipped in into one of her pockets, after unloading the pocket's previous contents into one of the cubby boxes on the wall. She pulled the key out of the wall and the viewer faded off. She stuck the key in her pocket, left her room and headed for the second floor.

There were about a dozen other people milling around the common room when Jack arrived. She guessed that some of them weren't actual newcomers, but she had to wonder about the number of people at the complex. Were there really ten or more new members every day or did she just happen to show up on an orientation day? And if there really were so many people interested in the Red, how come she had never heard of them until a week ago?

Jack hung around the back of the room, watching the others. There were some chairs set up facing a lectern at the front of the room. Slowly, people began to take the seats and Jack slipped into a chair in the last row. One of the people up front, an older looking woman, walked up to the lectern and cleared her throat.

"Hi, everyone, can we get settled?" she said, "I'd like to get started as soon as we can." The group quickly stopped chatting and gave her their attention. "Thanks, everyone. My name is Alaina and I'm going to be your guide for this orientation to the Red. Obviously, you all know something about us and what we do, or you wouldn't be here, but there's always more to know. Also, you'll want to learn about the various programs available here at the compound and I can help you with that too. If anyone has any questions before we get started, go ahead and ask."

Everyone was silent and most people shifted in their seats a little. It was strange being in an environment where the other participants could see each other or that you couldn't control the image they saw. Jack was pleased to see that she wasn't the only one uncomfortable with the situation and began to believe that she might make it through the weekend without being exposed as a fraud after all.

Alaina continued on. "Okay, then, let's start with an overview of the Red way of life. Of course, we are a loosely grouped collection of individuals whose views run along a continuum. At one end are the folks who are drawn to the Red because they oppose the typical modern way of life, others simply think that people ought to question their surroundings more often and they want to be part of actions and events that help to shine a light on certain aspects of society.

"At the other end are those of us who do not participate in specific types of human/machine integration. Those Reds who subscribe to this more radical doctrine remove any systems which allow direct machine access, such as implants to connect to everywherenet or the identity chips in your palms." She held up her left hand and a small gasp escaped a few of the participants, even though it was a demonstration, not an example.

Alaina laughed, "Don't worry, there is no dogma here. No one has to do anything, the whole point of the Red is to get away from the strict rules and regulations that society has placed on us all. Like I said, some of us are just here for the art. But you need to know that some of the people you will meet at the compound have strong opinions about integrated technology and we all strive to be inclusive. Therefore, you cannot assume that everyone here is able to be connected wirelessly, or that everyone is chipped. Many people here are not. That's why you'll find keys and cables used here more often than anything else.

"This brings me to the first thing you'll need to learn about staying at the compound. Keys." She pulled a plastic stick out of her pocket that was similar to the one Jack had been given by the surly front desk clerk. "You all have been given a key to get to your room. This key is your token for the whole complex — it's the equivalent of your identity chip. We do not read identity chips here, so access to the various buildings and courses is determined by your key. If you lose it, it will be a big hassle, so keep a close eye on it. Many of our new folks tie it to themselves." Alaina pulled out a tangled mess of red lanyards.

Most of the participants giggled, but a good number of them rose to take a lanyard. Jack joined the group who took the strings, not trusting herself to remember the small key. She affixed the key to one end of the lanyard, then slipped it over her head, stuffing the key between her sweater and t-shirt. "Okay, one last bit of housekeeping before we get into the meat of it all. You all should have been assigned a room and you've noticed there's no kitchen. We all eat together in a communal hall in the main building. There are a number of sittings for each meal, which you can learn from the viewer in your room."

She proceeded to explain how the viewer worked and the information available from Red Five. There were schedules, program outlines and you could sign up to attend events through the viewer. Then, Alaina got to the part that was the least interesting, but in some way the most important.

"Now, many of you are probably wondering how much this is going to cost," she said, "and the answer is both nothing and a lot. The Red complex is run by donations and volunteers; there is no cost to stay here and learn." The group erupted into murmurs of shock and delight. "However," Alaina said, "everyone who stays here is expected to contribute to the community. On your viewer you will also find work schedules. For ever two programs you attend, you will have to put in a shift of work. There's lots to do, so you will all surely find something suitable." She explained that the Red also accepted financial donations, but that money could not be used to get out of work.

There was a bit more explanation of the way things worked and some chit chat among the participants, but Jack wanted to get back to her room to check out the schedule. She had no idea how she was going to go about finding out about the human programming work; she doubted there would be a course on Advanced Consciousness Control. She left the orientation session as soon as it seemed politic to do so and headed back up to 10734.

SEVENTEEN

JACK STUCK HER key in the viewer's slot and when the friendly voice said, "Hello, boxenjester, how can I help you?" she replied, "Show me the meal schedule for today." She saw that there was a late sitting that evening for dinner and asked the viewer to remind her ten minutes before it was time to go. She then asked to see the schedule of classes for the next two days.

There was a huge selection of programs available and at first Jack had trouble believing that it was possible for even a large and well organized group to deliver this many courses and workshops over two days. Then, on closer inspection, she realized that only a small portion of the offerings were live, in-person events. Most of the programs were downloadable tutorials or immersive simulations. For a group that had a strong anti-progress component this seemed odd, but Jack suspected that few of the people involved in the beginner's events fell into this category anyway.

She looked at the course listings and sorted it by live events. Her eye had caught a few interesting choices among the simulations, but Jack wasn't here to actually learn about how to recruit performance artists, an overview of the various law enforcement agencies with the major firms, or advanced body-painting techniques. She was here to talk to the actual people running this outfit, so she had to surround herself with living, breathing bodies.

She picked a couple of selections at random and the viewer automatically prompted her to sign up for a work shift. She looked through the options and saw that there were spaces available for people with programming skills. She immediately put her name in for a couple of shifts there and the viewer shifted back to her schedule, showing options for four more courses. Jack filled these new slots with more in person events and by the time she was done she was registered for almost all of the physical space courses.

She finished up just as Red Five reminded her that her meal sitting was about to begin, so she pulled her key out of the slot and headed out of her room. She walked over to the main building and all of a sudden realized that there was so much open space here that she could see the sky. It was dull grey, but there were pinpricks of light showing through. She wondered if any of them were stars, or if they were all satellites for everywherenet, surveillance or internal firm communications. She was walking along, craning her neck up to see the lights in the sky when she literally bumped into someone.

She jumped back and began to apologize. The other person, a tall, blonde man in a one piece suit of a soft dark material, laughed and said, "Don't worry about it. I did the same thing the first time I was here."

Jack flushed despite herself and said, "I guess it's no shame to be a noob."

"Nope," he said, "everyone is at some point." He stuck his right hand out for her to shake. "I'm Lars," he said and they shook hands as Jack introduced herself. "Oh," he said, pausing to pull a small device with a screen from a pocket and consulting it briefly. "I think I have you in my Introduction to Body Work session tomorrow."

Jack smiled shyly, not remembering any of the courses for which she had registered. "Could be," she said, opting for as much honesty as she thought she could get away with, "I'm a little overwhelmed at the moment and it's hard to keep it all straight in my mind."

"Well, you're registered for the right class, then," Lars said with a wide smile, "after all the augmentation we're used to, we're all pretty handicapped without the 'nets and a smart system integrating it all. Hell, even I don't trust my memory." He waved the device in his hand at Jack. "You'll find the class interesting, I think," he continued.

"I hope so," Jack said, smiling. "Were you heading into the meal hall?"

"I was," he said, turning toward the door of the main building, "shall we eat together?"

"I'd like that," Jack said, amazed at her good fortune to find someone whose brain she could pick for the next half hour. They entered the main building and climbed the large central staircase to the meal hall. The previous sitting was just finishing up, so Jack and Lars had to wait a while for a couple of seats to free up. When a table became available, they slipped in and sat down.

"So," Lars asked as they looked over the brief menu scrolling in the tabletop, "what brings you to the compound?" Jack knew that this question would come up and had prepared a response. She had hoped that the first time she tried out her answer it wouldn't be with a Red staffer, but maybe it was better to find out early if her cover was going to be blown.

She had decided to go with the premise that the closer she stuck to the truth, the better off she would be. She explained that she had been a frequenter of the underground boards and had heard of a few of the Red actions there. "Eventually I wangled an invitation to an open house party — that was just last weekend, actually." Lars smiled and indicated that she should continue. "I went and really got interested in what the people there were doing, but also some of the other things going on elsewhere. One of the organizers suggested I come here and, well, here I am." Jack smiled in what she hoped was a winning way.

Lars nodded and said, "That's a pretty common story. Most of our people found us by just noticing things and getting interested. We're not really popular as such, but as you can see, we get a lot of interest." Jack looked around and saw a good three dozen people sitting around the tables in the room and of course, this was only about a third of the people attending the complex. She shook her head in amazement and looked down at the menu scrolling on the table.

There weren't many choices, but Jack really wasn't picky. To her, nutrient bricks pretty much all tasted the same. She settled on something they were calling lentil casserole and waited for Lars to decide to see what he did. He pushed on a small pulsing light on the right side of the table, which stopped the scrolling, then tapped the table on the name of his choice. The menu flashed once and then disappeared. Jack did the same and poked her index finger on the "n" of lentil. "They're pretty quick," Lars said and sure enough, in less than five minutes two steaming bowls slid down from the track in the wall next to the table. Lars lifted them off the small ledge and set them down on the table.

Jack looked in the bowl and wasn't sure what to say. The look on her face must have been obvious, because Lars said, "Oh, yeah, we serve real food here. Some Reds won't eat nutrient blocks and we have a small farm on the grounds, as well as shipments from friendly farms all over Namerica. I hope you like it." He scooped up a spoonful of stew and chewed it thoughtfully. Jack was still dumbfounded. She tentatively took a bite of the casserole. It was amazing, so full of flavour and textures, like some kind of magic in her mouth. She would have happily spent a day's pay for this meal and they were giving it away.

They ate in silence, Lars noticing that Jack was too engrossed in the meal to make conversation. After they were finished, he said, "I guess you liked it." She nodded, still savouring the tastes lingering in her mouth. "There aren't that many people who can cook anymore, but the ones who can seem to like it a lot and we get more than our fair share of cooks. So we always seem to manage to get good food out here. It's a definite perk for the full time folks, let me tell you."

They got up and headed for the door. "So," Jack asked, "do you live here?"

"I'm here most of the time," Lars said, "sometimes I go back to Europe to see family, but I'd say my home is here at the compound. I've been teaching and living here for about two years now."

"Wow," Jack said. "That's a long time. I didn't realize that the organization had been active this long."

"Yeah, we're not as well known as we could be I suppose," Lars said, "but we've been around in some fashion or another for a good bit longer than I've been here." They left the hall, walking down the stairs and out the front door of the building. At the crossroads of the walking paths, they stopped and looked up at the sky again.

"It was nice talking to you, Jack," Lars said, beginning to turn away from her. "I'll see you in class tomorrow."

"Thanks," she replied and turned toward the building her room was in. She walked toward her room almost in a daze. As she stuck her key in the slot by her door, she began to realize that she was starting to like it here. The combination of open skies and real food were powerful and she reminded herself of Estella Rowan, Mario Keating and who knows how many others who would never see sky of any kind again. She made sure the door to her room was locked, then stripped and showered. She lay in the small bed, thinking about the things she had heard, wondering if she was wrong. Maybe the Red weren't behind what happened to Rowan and the others. Maybe she was off on a wild goose chase — after all it was completely circumstantial evidence that led her here.

Hell, she thought, I'm no expert on identifying code authors. What was I thinking; imagining that I could guess who was behind it all? Maybe they really are as nice as they seem here. Maybe…

She fell asleep wondering.

• • •

The next morning Red Five woke her up with a simple musical alarm. She woke slowly, almost naturally, after about eight hours of sleep. She got up and got dressed, then headed to the hall for breakfast. She ate alone this time, as did most of the other people in the room. After breakfast, she went back to her room to check her schedule. She found the place her first session was being held and took an image of the map in case she got lost.

She only had a few minutes to get there in time and hurried down the paths. She found the building without too much difficulty and entered the assigned room. About a half dozen other participants were already there and Lars was at the front of the room chatting with one of them. He saw Jack and smiled and she returned the grin. She picked a chair next to a woman with flaming magenta hair and a pair of implanted horns on top of her head. Jack figured that she must be fairly young; that trend was hot again and most of the people who had it done the first time around had had them removed by now.

"Hi," the horned girl said, "I'm Susanna." She stuck out her hand and they shook.

"I'm Jack, nice to meet you," Jack answered. They sat there, neither of them knowing what to say. Before either of them found a way to break the silence, Lars cleared his throat and began the session.

"Hi, everyone," he said, "I'm Lars and I'll be leading this course, Introduction to Body Work. Now, because this is an introduction, I'm going to assume that all of you are new to the complex and maybe even to the Red, is that right?" He looked around the room at the participants and was met with a stony silence. "I'll take that as agreement," Lars said to a few chuckles, "and take this opportunity to point out the only thing we really need to get out of this class — we have grown accustomed to using our systems and the nets for communication, so we tend not to remember that our bodies are means of communication also. When we react or don't react with our faces or our postures, we are telling everyone around us all kinds of information.

"Let's talk about that moment we just had," he said, sitting on a chair at the front of the room. "And while we're at it, we can introduce ourselves. I'll start. I'm Lars, I've been involved with the Red for several years and I've been living and working here at the compound for about two years now. I noticed that when I asked you all a question and none of you did anything, it felt like no-one was listening to me." He turned to the person closest to him, a man with gold coloured hair, clothes and skin. "What's your name and what did you notice?"

The participant said, "I'm known as golden," at that, some of the others giggled, "and I noticed that I didn't know how to answer. I could have answered for myself, but how do you answer a question that's directed to everyone? So I just did nothing."

"That's good," Lars said, "a good observation about how that happened. Next," he said, gesturing to Susanna, "what did you notice." She talked about how she is not used to being addressed as part of a group and didn't know how to respond. As a group they continued to talk about how they rarely encounter situations where body language is relevant, let alone necessary. Lars taught them simple gestures, how to hold your body to indicate comfort or distress and how to notice facial expressions and simple cues from others.

They discussed how what once had been perceived as simple courtesy had all but disappeared from normal conduct, how conducing relationships without ever seeing the other party was the norm and how the body was seen as an unfortunate encumbrance by many people. Jack thought that the class seemed to be more about talking about how the world of flesh was perceived and used than it was about learning specific skills, but either way it was actually pretty interesting.

By lunch time Jack had completely forgotten about what she was really doing there at the complex and instead was focussed on all the ideas she had heard and discussed in the morning's class. She walked to the main building with Susanna, where they continued talking about the concepts of the morning's session. At lunch, as they were discussing whether negating the value of the body was a way for firms to control the workers, Jack had a mental image of Estella

Rowan and seriously wondered for the first time what was happening to her body. Her mind was gone, but her body had to be somewhere; even if she was dead, her body had to be somewhere.

Why had no-one noticed her? Noticed either her missing body or her body where it didn't belong. How could someone just disappear?

OOIIO

THE BLACKOUTS CONTINUE; they are more frequent now, at least one a day. And when I dream, I dream such things I cannot believe and I fear they are not dreams, these images I see in the night. They seem more like memories but when I wake I can only remember the sensations, the emotions, not the actions.

I can feel them coming on, those moments when I am no longer myself. It feels like a download but more invasive somehow, like sex without the pleasure. I fight them, the blackouts, but it only makes the pain worse. And when I come back, it is like a hangover magnified, the pain, disorientation and tension.

I don't know how to fight this any more. I have to end this, but what can I do? What can I do?

EIGHTEEN

THE THOUGHT OF Estella Rowan reminded Jack of her purpose at the compound and renewed her resolve to find out who was behind the consciousness programs. She had her first work shift after lunch and was hopeful that whatever they would have her doing as a programmer would shed some light on the situation. She agreed to meet Susanna for dinner at the middle sitting and headed off to her room to find out where she was supposed to go for her work shift.

The morning class had been interesting and compelling, but now as she walked all the way back to her room to find out a piece of information that would take just a second on the nets to retrieve, she was becoming less enamoured with the whole Red philosophy. It was nice to play historical and pretend not to have everywherenet or integrated systems, but there was a good reason everyone adopted those technologies in the first place.

Jack entered her room and stuck her key into the viewer. She found the location of the programmers' lab and took an image of it. She had a few minutes to spare and tried to call up a mashup of the whole complex map and her schedule for the rest of her stay. Amazingly, the viewer complied and she gratefully took an image of the map showing everywhere she needed to be and when she needed to be there. It wasn't as good as having a system do it all for her, but if she found a few spare minutes she could program her local system to remind her where she was going every time she had a new session.

She yanked the key from the viewer and headed back outside. She walked briskly to the programmers' lab. When she arrived, she met a handful of other obvious noobs and a couple of people who were clearly going to be showing them the ropes. Jack was curious to discover what they even did, since it seemed like the Red tried to avoid systems and the nets as much as possible. A few other people arrived and one of the staffers addressed the group.

"Hi, everyone," the tall nondescript woman said, "You can call me Luj. I'm going to show you all around our systems and get you all set up with jobs to do. These tasks might not be glamourous, but they need doing and you all need stuff to do, so there you have it."

"Now, you will have noticed that we don't tend to use wireless here very much — some of the people here aren't equipped for it. Most of us in the labs do use it, though there are ways for anyone who isn't chipped. Is there anyone who would prefer a hard wired line into the system?" The members of the group looked around at each other, with looks of confusion on their faces. Jack found a use for some of what she had learned in the morning and spoke up.

"I don't think any of us prefer a hard wire, since it looks like most of us don't know what you're talking about." Luj laughed and a few of the other noobs made affirming noises.

"Fair enough," Luj said, "well, I'd better start there." She moved over to a workstation and pulled out a long cable from the wall. "Most of the Reds who don't use wireless still use the nets at least some of the time. They get implants where we all have our wireless nodes that allow a cable to be plugged in."

"They what?" one of Jack's fellow noobs asked, alternately shocked and amazed.

Luj smiled patiently and explained that they get in input jack implanted in their heads where the rest of us have wireless nodes implanted. Then, when they want to connect to the network, they stick the prong end of the cable into the jack and away they go. "Eww," said the same person who originally questioned the process, "that's nasty, sticking shit in yer head."

"It's a lot less nasty than implanting foreign bodies in there permanently," said the other staffer, a soft-spoken man who looked older than anyone Jack had ever seen. "At least I can take the shit out of my head whenever I want to." He turned away from the group and Jack could see a small black artificial looking patch just behind and below his left ear.

"Okay, everyone, I think we've beaten this dead horse into the ground," Luj said, herding the group toward a set of chairs and viewers. "These will be your workstations and you can log in wirelessly here, just flip this switch to the on position," she pointed out a lighted button next to the viewer, "and insert your key for authentication. Then you'll be on the system with the basic permissions we've given you as new users. If you'll each take a station and log in, you'll get your assignments for the shift."

Jack grabbed a chair in the middle and completed the login procedure. She was greeted by the same friendly voice as the viewer, but this time it identified itself as Red Three. It gave Jack the promised boring task, reviewing code for a new version of the scheduling module of Red Five. It wasn't programming Intelligent Agents, but it was better than any of the other jobs on offer. Plus, Jack got to poke around the internal Red system while she was there.

It was very much like a cross between a typical firm's network and an individual's local system. The scheduling process was by far the majority of the system and the most collaborative. However, there were user accounts with backup storage and she noticed that there were at least two other systems outside the one in which she was working. She suspected that users with higher permissions could access those systems and that was exactly where she wanted to be.

It wasn't going to happen on this shift, though, since she just managed to poke around a little bit and review her assignment before the friendly voice told her that she was done for the day. Jack logged off Red Three and pulled up the map from her local system. She had about half an hour before she was scheduled for a short course on Common Lies We All Believe, And Who's Behind Them.

She left the labs and decided to take a quick stroll around the compound. She headed to the area behind the main building and the programmers' labs, where according to her map, the more seasoned Reds went about their business. There were a few people milling about and they certainly seemed more familiar with their surroundings than most of the people Jack had seen in the noobs' area. She found a central location with a bench and sat down, just letting the activity of the space flow around her.

She started paying attention to the little things about the people walking around her, the small differences. She noticed that a couple of people had the same kind of jacks in their heads as the quiet fellow at the programmers' lab. There were a few people who seemed to have done something strange to their left hands — the thumbs seemed to stick out at a funny angle. And Jack was convinced that one person was missing a left hand entirely. She was starting to wonder if she was seeing things that weren't there and decided it must be time to head to her next session. As she walked to her next class, she found herself looking more closely than usual at the limbs and ears of the people she passed.

She found her way to the meeting room for her next session and listened while an earnest speaker explained that firms existed only to make money and that they treated people the same way they treated any other asset they owned. Jack was amazed that this was news to anyone, but she had been working for the firms for three quarters of her life and had seen that attitude first hand. The speaker talked about some specific instances and highlighted those cases where people were cast aside like last year's chair or even where people died. Of course the law, such as it was, was made by the firms and backed up any action they took so long as it didn't interfere with another firm's business.

Some of the participants were shocked, but Jack was surprised that so few people knew the law. Individuals had stopped having rights outside of what their employment contracts included when she was a kid; maybe younger folks just didn't know what they were missing since they had never had it.

After a few more examples of old news, Jack tuned the speaker out and started planning how she would crack into the higher levels of the Red system. She was pretty sure that getting into the higher level systems would be fairly easy for her, the problem was making sure she didn't get caught. She thought that since they relied on physical keys as their primary authentication method, that she might be able to mask her identity that way somehow.

She spent the rest of the session planning her attack and when it was over she walked out of the room more or less in a daze. She headed back to the main hall and her dinner date with Susanna. Jack found her waiting at the entrance to the building and they walked into the dining area together. Jack asked Susanna how her session had gone.

"It was pretty jazz," Susanna said, grinning widely, "the guy was talking about how the ident chips we have track us all our lives and limit our freedoms. He was all about how we are tagged at birth then sold to the firms as if we were just another piece of gear."

"My session was pretty similar," Jack said, scanning today's dinner options. "It just wasn't focussed specifically on the identity chips."

"Well, mine was about why you should dig your own chip out," Susanna answered, "so that's why the focus was there." Jack was glad they hadn't gotten their meals yet, because she was sure she would have choked.

"Dig them out, yourself?" she asked incredulously.

"Yeah," Susanna said, picking the soup and rice combo, "a bunch of Reds removed their chips themselves. That's why you see some of the old timers with fucked up hands." She leaned in conspiratorially and lowered her voice. "Some of them, in the early days, just cut off their entire hands. They were a little whacked, I think, but supposedly that was before it was well known exactly where the chips were."

"Holy shit," Jack said. "That's so fucked up." She paused and picked something off the menu she had never heard of before.

"I know," Susanna said, sounding almost in awe of the whole concept. "I wouldn't have the cojones to whack off my hand, would you?"

"Hell no," Jack said, "nor would I want to. That's way too extreme for me."

"Yeah," Susanna said. "Though if I might get it done surgically. It's not as jazz as doing it solo with a pocket laser, but whatever. At least it wouldn't hurt."

"Are you serious?" Jack exclaimed. "That's way more of a big deal than a tat or..." her gaze strayed to the top of Susanna's head, "horns or something. That's a permanent lifestyle choice. You could never get a normal job again, never get a normal apartment for chrissakes. I don't think you can get a new chip all that easily, you know."

"I know," Susanna pouted, "and I'm not saying I'm going to do it for sure, but I'm thinking about it." The food arrived on the track on the wall and they took their bowls and began to eat. Jack was again stupefied by the tastes of the fresh food, while Susanna seemed to be having trouble with her meal.

"What's wrong?" Jack asked in between bites.

"It's just so... strong," Susanna said, her nose wrinkling in distaste. "I'm not used to this kind of food. It's weird."

"Whatever," Jack said, decided to spend the time enjoying the meal rather than arguing. Jack savoured her meal while Susanna chased hers around the bowl. When Jack was done, she asked, "You gonna eat that?" Susanna shook her head and Jack grabbed the bowl lustily and finished Susanna's portion. After she was done — maybe she was filled with magnanimity as well as food — she said, "I've got a few meal bars in my room, you can have them if you want."

Susanna smiled and said, "Thanks. I know I should just get used to it, but it's just too weird. I'd never had real food before I got here." Jack pitied the girl, but was happy enough to offload her bricks of nutrient laden sawdust in exchange for Susanna's soup. They got up to leave the room and head back to Jack's room, when Susanna suggested they hit the bar after.

"There's a bar?" Jack asked.

"Yup" Susanna said, "a bunch of the people here don't do substances, but there's a bar for the rest of us. That stuff costs money, though. I hope that's okay."

"That's fine," Jack said, already salivating at the thought of a beer. They walked to Jack's room, where she gave Susanna the food bricks she had brought with her. The two then walked over to the back of the main building and through an unmarked doorway. "They don't seem to want to advertise this place, do they," Jack asked.

"It seems like there's a lot around here they want you to just stumble over," Susanna said as they entered the dark room. "I think it might be a community building thing — you have to talk to people to find out what's going on."

"You could be on to something," Jack said, "I'm sure glad we talked about this, let me tell you." She grinned and they walked up to the bar itself. It was a long sheet of metal, not unlike the tracks in the meal hall. There was a human behind the bar and he asked them what they wanted.

"I'll take a beer," Jack said.

"Do you want a regular brew, or real beer?" the bartender asked.

"Uh, how much does real beer cost," Jack asked, then before the bartender could answer, she thought better of the question. "Never mind the cost, just give me one." The barman smiled and pulled a pint of dark liquid from the old fashioned tap on the bar. He named the price, which was high, but Jack was perfectly happy to pay. After confirming that she was wirelessly enabled, the bartender flipped on a wireless connection and Jack paid. Susanna ordered a drink Jack knew consisted primarily of THC.

They took their drinks to a nearby ledge and looked around. The room was dark with occasional strobes and other dim lights. Music was playing fairly loudly, but no one was dancing, though there was an open area in the middle of the space. There were maybe thirty people in the place, just chatting and drinking. And one of them had a big black ball instead of a right eye.

NINETEEN

JACK DIDN'T KNOW what to do. It was BlackEye for sure, chatting with some dour looking guy just two tables over. It was the first she had seen of him and although she had imagined before she arrived that he would be leading the group in some kind of bizarre incantation three times a day, once she had been here for a while the community nature of the group made her doubt even the existence of a leader. Of course, leaders aren't always of the "do it my way or get out" variety and she noticed that everyone else in the bar deferred to BlackEye when they interacted with him.

"Do you know who that guy is?" she asked Susanna, who was already starting to get an unfocussed look about her.

"Which guy?" she asked after a brief pause to understand the question.

"The one-eyed man with the hair wings. Over there," Jack jerked her head in the direction of the table. Susanna looked over and studied the two men carefully for some time before answering.

"Nope," she said, "I've never seen him before." She pulled out one of Jack's meal bars, opened it up and started to eat small bits of it. Jack took a sip of the beer and was momentarily distracted from BlackEye. The drink was full of flavour and a slightly harsh taste as well. Jack could now understand Susanna's difficulty with real food, although she was enjoying the new taste of her drink. She had a few more sips of the heady brew and noticed Lars walk in the door. He saw her and Susanna and headed over to their table.

"Well, I see it didn't take you long to find out some of our secrets," he said, grinning at the two women. Susanna looked at him more or less blankly, while Jack smiled and told him that Susanna had found it and brought her along. "I've never had real beer before," she said, wanting to share the experience, "this is fantastic."

"I like it myself," Lars said and excused himself to get one of his own. By the time he returned, Jack recognized the opportunity she had.

She decided to stick with the as much honesty as possible plan and said, "At the open house I was at last weekend, someone from here was speaking over the nets. I think it was that guy over there," she tried to subtly point out BlackEye. "Who is he?"

"That's Rackham," Lars said. He took a long drink of his own real beer, then set the glass down on the ledge. Susanna was still munching on her food brick as Lars continued. "He was one of the founders of the Red. A cracker of the old school, who got booted out of the firm he worked for after some scandal or another. There are plenty of stories about what happened to his eye, but the truth is that he tells a different one each time someone asks. He's hard as nails and the only reason that the compound ever succeeded.

"He holds most of the extreme views: no wireless, real food only, no implants of any kind — hell they say he even interfaces with the network using viewers and some kind of writing device rather than a cable. But he is adamant that the Red accommodate everyone. He's scary as hell, but we wouldn't be anywhere without him – I swear he makes infrastructure out of thin air. He built this place out of nothing and sometimes I think he keeps it together by the sheer force of his personality." Lars paused for breath and Jack though she saw a glint in his eye. "You want me to introduce you?"

"Christ," Jack said, taking a swig of her beer, "after a description like that I'm more inclined to turn tail and run the other direction as soon as I see him."

"Oh, it'll be fine," Lars said, "he's really nice to the noobs. Come on." He started toward BlackEye/Rackham and Jack felt compelled to follow. As they approached the table, the two men stopped talking and looked their way. Rackham was old - Jack gathered as much from the brief biography Lars had provided. But in person he actually looked old and that was maybe more unusual than the matte black orb in place of his right eye. The other man at the table was one of the people Jack had seen earlier with the hands. Or, in his case, the lack of a hand. "Rackham, Morty, this is Jack," Lars introduced her to the two men at the table, "she's one of the new folks who was in my session this morning." The man he introduced as Morty gave a vague smile then looked away as if he were shy or demented. Rackham grinned and stuck out a large hand toward Jack. She shook his hand and smiled back.

"I saw you at one of the smaller gatherings last weekend," she said, "and I just had to come out here. This is one hell of a place you've got here."

"Well, thank you, my dear," Rackham said, picking up his dark drink and sucking back nearly a quarter of the contents of the large glass. "We try to get the word out as best we can. I hope you're enjoying it here, but more importantly that you are finding what you're looking for. As much as I appreciate all the work everyone does for the cause, the truth of the matter is that people need the Red more than the Red needs people. Isn't that right, Lars?"

Rackham slapped the smaller man hard on the back and Lars sputtered slightly as he answered that he supposed that was true. "Damn rights it's true," Rackham answered and Jack noticed that he was slurring his words a little. Shit, she thought, crazy and drunk. That's a great combination. "It's all a great circle, people." He waved his large hands in the air, demonstrating the circle. "We do what we do for the benefit of the others. And we need people to do what we do. But if there were no one to benefit from our work, we wouldn't need to do it and then we wouldn't need the people." He brought his hands down to the ledge with rather a lot of force and glared at his audience. "Is this sinking in at all?" He was beginning to shout, though Jack thought it was more of a volume control issue rather than anger that caused his voice to rise.

"I think I get it," she said, emboldened perhaps by a realization that he was human after all or perhaps by half a pint of real beer. "The movement exists for the benefit of people. When the administration of the organization becomes more important than actually helping people, then the priorities are obviously all wrong."

"Close enough," Rackham said and drank most of the rest of his drink. He signalled the barman for another and said, "Pretty damn good for a noob, I'd have to say." He polished off his drink and said, "Well, it's been nice talking to you all," and turned away from them. It was an obvious cue that the conversation was over and they should go away. Jack and Lars went back to the table where Susanna was still sitting, enjoying her own little world.

"So, that's our Rackham," Lars said. "Like I said, scary as hell but a real leader."

"He sure is something," Jack said, trying to reconcile his words with the mind control programs. It didn't fit, but Jack knew that words aren't worth that much in the grand scheme of things. She drank the rest of her beer quietly and saw that Lars was also lost in thought. She looked at him, as if for the first time. He was brooding at that moment, probably trying to think if there was a way that meeting could have gone better. His long face was pursed in thought but his skin was unlined and soft-looking. He was pale, with light hair and eyes and Jack imagined that he would be the kind of man that would have filled the ancient Nordic romantic novels. He had no augmentation that Jack could see, including a cable shunt, so she figured him for one of the moderates.

She watched the strobes reflect off his skin and realized for the first time that she was attracted to him. Maybe it was that he was the first person to talk to her, or maybe her encounter at the party the previous weekend had awakened desires for flesh sex she never knew she had. Or, maybe it was the strong home brew beer. Whatever it was, she knew she either had to make a move or move on. As she was deciding, Susanna came out of her stupor and announced that she was getting a bit freaked out and had to go back to her room. They said farewell and she headed out of the bar, leaving Jack alone with Lars. They looked at each other for a while in silence, then Jack made up her mind. "Show me your room?" she asked.

They left the bar and walked back to his room in the staff quarters. It was no different from hers except for a larger work area near the viewer. When they arrived, Lars produced a large bottle of ale from a cupboard near the entrance. They shared the bottle, as he set the viewer to play some soft instrumental music. They didn't speak once, even after the bottle was empty and their clothes were on the floor next to their tangled bodies. Jack had to admit to herself that Lars knew his subject and she got more than an introduction on how to use her body that night.

• • •

Jack didn't return to her room and instead shared the small bed with Lars. The alarm woke them in the morning and they smiled at each other after a brief moment of awkwardness. They showered together and walked to the meal hall. Only after having the first few bites of breakfast did they speak.

"I guess that was the intermediate lesson," Jack said, lightly, grinning.

Lars was more earnest. "I don't usually do that," he said, awkwardly, but also smiling. "I'm not one to see students as opportunities. I realize that physical intimacy has repercussions that aren't always evident and I want to be clear that I don't expect anything of you because of last night."

Jack laughed. "Don't worry," she said, trying for a world weary air, "It's not like I haven't had flesh sex before. I'm not going to make things difficult for you, it's okay. I do like talking to you, though, you have been very helpful. Can we have dinner tonight, if I promise to keep my hands to myself?" She smiled disarmingly and Lars finally allowed himself a grin.

"Sure," he said. "I'm just cognizant of my role as a teacher and how those power constructs can complicate matters."

Jack laughed and shook her head, finishing her breakfast. "You're funny as hell, Lars," she said, as she rose from the table and got ready to head back to her room. "For all your freedom, you're as trapped as the rest of us. I'll see you at the bar before dinner?" She asked and they agreed on a time. She left the table and walked back to her room. She changed clothes and left for her first class of the day, a study of community building.

The content of the morning class was way over Jack's head and she couldn't even tune it out because it was almost all class participation. The lecturer started the session by earnestly talking about the value of communities of like-minded people and passed out the link to an online course that taught how to set up a local chapter of the Red. She gave a brief overview of the basic elements of organizing a group of vaguely like-minded but probably significantly disparate people.

Jack was starting to doze off when the tone of the class shifted radically and the participation began. She had to partner with another class member and do some kind of idea-sharing exercise, there were trust-building games and Jack thought there was more touching going on in this session than the body work class yesterday. If Lars thinks there's some kind of special intimacy in body contact, Jack thought, he'd better steer clear of this group.

After what felt like an eternity, the class was over. Jack was amazed when she realized that it had been one of the short sessions and that she was due to report to the programmers' lab for a work session before lunch. She made a beeline for the lab and was one of the first people to arrive for this shift. The shift captain assigned her to work with debugging some experimental code for regulating the water supply, but she managed to trade shifts with a shy old timer who was scheduled to set up new users and found it a painfully boring task.

Jack hoped that she would be able to set up a dummy user for herself to use while she was sneaking around. She set to adding the group of new users and found that there seemed to be a simple process for the task. She also discovered that the physical key they all carried, a token she had assumed was a necessary step in the authentication process, was really just the delivery system for a chunk of encrypted signed code. Sure, if she was trying to get into the viewer in her room she would need a key since there was no other delivery mechanism. But in the labs there was wireless, so she could just download the authentication code for the dummy user to her local system and use it when she tried to log in. At least, she hoped it would work that way.

She finished the first list of new users, then pulled out a list of user upgrades that were waiting for another staffer. She gave it a try, but her permissions were too low to enable her to perform the upgrade. So much for making a higher level user for herself. She went back to the new users list and added a dummy identity. No alarms went off, even when she downloaded the generated key to her local system rather than moving it to the central key creation folder.

She noticed that she was flushed and sweating. She had always had a visceral response to doing things she knew could land her in the soup; it was one of the reasons she had decided to stay on the easy side of the law. She deliberately slowed her breathing down and was just about looking and feeling normal when the shift ended. The shy guy who'd switched shifts with her met her on the way out and thanked her again for saving him a couple of hours of mind numbing boredom.

"No problem," she said, trying to control her autonomic physical responses, "any time." They went their separate ways as Jack headed for the meal hall. She sat at one of the stools that was just under a section of the track and hoped no one came to sit next to her. She had another work shift immediately after lunch then an optional short class before her late dinner date with Lars. She was hoping to get into the higher level systems in her next shift, then depending on what she found, who knew what would happen.

As she ate she pulled up her cracker's tool kit and looked through all the utilities. From what she had seen so far, the local system here seemed to be organized in a fashion pretty similar to the other systems Jack had used. She figured that her tools ought to be able to crack into the upper echelons of the system and that she would be able to access all the files. Her only worry was that the false user she had created would be too obvious and that she wouldn't be able to cover her tracks. There wasn't anything else she could do at this point to make the process go more smoothly, except abandon the attempt. So, she ate her lunch and prepared herself for the afternoon's attack.

TWENTY

THE SYSTEM WAS different. At first Jack nearly panicked when she realized that her three D rendering engine couldn't handle the configuration of the Red system and showed her nothing but an empty blue void. But, after backing out and viewing the system using her terminal emulator, Jack was able to navigate the system. She got a feel for the layout, finding her way through the hierarchical structure. Eventually, she banged up against the point where her dummy user's permissions ended.

She breathed deeply and turned away from her task for a moment. She had an assignment from the shift captain and she guessed that if it didn't get done they might come checking up on her. She pulled out her bag of tricks and quickly modified a script to do her job for her. She got it running under her own user id and set it to notify her when it was done so she could check the work. She switched back to the dummy id and held her breath.

She started cracking into the higher level systems. It was slow going, because she was trying to be careful about leaving traces. Occasionally she would switch back to her real id and check on the script, but it seemed to be doing fine. After what seemed like an eternity but was really more like six or seven minutes, she was in. All the way up to Red One, the highest access level. She was somewhat surprised to see that it was mostly just separate repositories for each of the staffers.

She opened one at random and saw viewer logs, lesson plans, personal journals, the usual stuff you would find on a personal system. She went straight to Rackham's area and started poking around.

She found the text of a few lectures, an accounting file and a list of goals for the movement. She opened the list of goals and started to read. It was clearly a public relations piece, since there was nothing earth shattering on there and the tone didn't sound anything like the man she had talked to the previous night at the bar. It didn't even sound like the speech she had heard at the open house.

She realized that she wasn't going to find the evidence just lying around marked with an X. She needed the equivalent of a map. She switched back to her own user account to check on the script and got an idea. She still had a copy of the code she had found at the Buyside Client Delivery System and she could just write a script to compare the code fragment to the contents of all the files on the system. She found a search script in her local systems and began modifying it to suit the Red system.

She tested it a few times on the lower level system, looking for known strings and it seemed to be pretty successful at finding what she was looking for. She input one of the code fragments from the Buyside raid and set the script to run over the entire Red One system. She knew it would take some time and switched back to her own account while she waited. The script for her assignment finished and she checked its work. It was perfectly fine; no one would ever know that Jack hadn't done it all by hand. She had to wonder why they didn't just use scripts for most of the work — it was a real waste of time having people do it manually.

As she was thinking of other ways to automate the various jobs that were assigned at the programmers' labs, her search script notified her that it had found a match. She felt her heartbeat quicken and sweat break out all over her body as if she had a fever. She swallowed hard and switched over to the dummy account. She opened up the matching file and saw that it was definitely one of the tools used to break into Buyside.

This was conclusive evidence. She hadn't been on a wild goose chase after all; her hunch about Rackham had paid off and she figured that it would be fairly easy now to prove that he was the one who was behind the mind control programs. She double checked and her script told her that this was the only match on the whole system, so it had to be him. Just to be sure, she ran the command to show which area the file was located in. And she nearly lost her lunch when she saw that it wasn't Rackham who had broken into Buyside; it was Lars.

• • •

Jack was stunned. Lars? Sure, she hardly knew the man and a few hours of grab-ass the night before didn't change that fact, but he seemed so... benign. How could anyone who taught ancient body language and wanted to talk about his feelings be responsible for the horrors she had seen? It didn't make sense, or maybe she just didn't want it to make sense. Maybe she was wrong, maybe this didn't prove anything. She wished she had never come here.

A chime sounded, indicating that her shift was almost over and it brought her mind back to reality. She had to be sure, so she took a risk and started a file dump of Lars' entire area to her local system. She had to turn off her automatic recording routine and trash some temp files to make room, but she was pretty sure she'd be able to get it all. The weight in her head as the download took place was painful, but she welcomed it. She knew the throbbing would end once the files were all received and hoped that the roiling feeling in her stomach would end as well. The chime for the end of her shift sounded, but she waited a few moments for the download to finish. She logged out of the system, not bothering to take the time to ensure that any traces of her visit were erased.

She left the labs in a daze and walked straight back to her room. Once inside, she took off her clothes and got into the shower. She set the shower to remain on until she turned it off manually and stayed under the water for a long time. She alternately tried to make herself not care about the situation, forget her relationship with Lars, minimize its significance — anything to get through the next few hours. Eventually she brought up the image of Estella Rowan's face. She focussed on the small knot of rage and pity that had built inside her since the moment she found Rowan's ravaged mind and finally shut off the water. She dried herself under the blower, left the bathroom and got into the small bed. She lay back, closed her eyes and started sifting through the files from Lars' system.

At first she tried to group them according to their titles, but quickly realized that as a basic security precaution he hadn't labeled any of them obviously, so she would have to scan through them all. Fine. She set to work. She sifted through his teaching schedule, a few academic-style essays regarding the loss of physicality in modern society and some of his correspondence with family in Europe. None of these files contained any hint of a reason for breaking into random systems, let alone an indication that he was behind the mind control program.

Then Jack came across some specs from the original European study with the bonobos and her heart sank. She realized she had again grown hopeful that she was wrong, that Lars wasn't the one. She scanned through the information and saw that he had filled the document with marginalia about adapting the tool to human use. Jack checked the author information and the annotations were all attributed to Lars. It was circumstantial evidence, but it was proof enough for Jack.

She kept looking though his files and found some strange documents labeled Beautiful Red. Most of the files were schematics about building huge racks of disk. She looked through them and saw that Lars was trying to get large quantities of disk networked together to run a program he was developing called the Maker. Jack ran a search and found the beginnings of the code for the Maker. She read through the code, expecting to see the mind control program. Instead, it seemed to be a fully recursive program that did nothing but analyze itself. Jack could see why you would need a lot of disk for it, but couldn't see any reason why you want to run such a program. It was unfinished and Jack could tell from the dates and the modifications that this fragment was the first version. There were indications that a subsequent version had been written, but she could find no copy of it among the files she had downloaded.

She found some more files tagged "BR" and quickly scanned through them. It was a strange mix of information. There were some more specs from the European chimpanzee study, several clippings from boards devoted to the creation and study of intelligent agents, some philosophical studies of sentience and old work on creating artificial intelligence. That last grouping was pretty strange. Long ago, scientists had concluded that intelligent agents could only ever achieve sentience though an evolutionary-type process — that only through learning could they become self aware. While it hadn't happened yet, this was the commonly accepted theory. But Lars had been collecting work from before that theory became common, designs for ways to create fully sentient machines from scratch.

Jack scanned through the documents, but there wasn't anything she found interesting there. It was just full of old theories that would interest a historian more than they would a programmer. She kept searching through the files she had taken, looking for connections, evidence, looking for answers. She skimmed over the names of the files and directories tagged "BR" again: ai/docs/, building_log, root_access_v2.6, sentience/docs, study_756/specs/, the_maker_vi.i. Her eye stumbled on what appeared to be a program — root access. She opened it up in her terminal emulator and started reading the code. She gasped, realizing that this was the mind control program.

She opened her eyes and sat up, gasping for breath. She had been looking through the files for about an hour and she needed water. She got out of the bed and grabbed a bottle from the cupboard. She drank it and put on some clothes. She walked around the small room, getting energy back into her body. This was it — the evidence she needed. She left her room and walked back to the programmers' lab, still gripping her water bottle as if she were trying to strangle it.

She arrived at the lab and snuck into one of the unused areas. There was a shift on, but it was a small crew working and Jack was pretty sure she hadn't been seen. She logged into the system using her dummy id and quickly got into Lars' directory. She dropped a script she had quickly written on the way over into the top level of his directory and backed out. Then she started looking for a way out of the local system and onto everywherenet. She wanted to contact someone, anyone, and tell them what she had found, but it soon became clear that the Red system was completely closed.

Frustrated but determined, she logged out of the system and snuck out of the building. She was supposed to be meeting Lars for drinks in half an hour. Part of her wanted to just leave now and turn him in to the authorities. But she had come so far and found so little; she needed to know why. She went straight to the bar and order a large very strong gin and tonic. She was halfway through the liquid courage, when he walked in.

She had planned all kinds of clever things to say, violence to perform and cutting looks to deliver, but when she saw him her first reaction was that she must have made some kind of mistake. He seemed so kind to people, so interested in their welfare and now he looked so happy to see her, that Jack had a hard time believing her own conclusions. He waved to her and gestured that he was going to the bar first. She nodded and drank more of her g & t, her well rehearsed lines dying unsaid in her mind.

He came to the table with a couple of real ales for them both and set them down. He leaned over to kiss her, but Jack put her hand on his chest, stopping him. "What's Beautiful Red?" she asked, her voice soft as she looked him in the eyes. His pupils dilated and he looked as if she had hit him in the stomach.

"What... how..." he stammered, "I, where did you hear that?

Jack swallowed hard. "I've been through your directory on Red One," she said, matter of factly. She sighed, air escaping her lungs as if she were deflating. "Just tell me and get it over with." Lars looked around him, as if preparing to run away, then Jack could tell he just gave up. He looked as if someone had let the air out of him as he sagged into his chair.

He took a large drink from his beer and said, "I was just in there dropping off some class notes. You're very good. I didn't notice a thing."

Jack closed her eyes, breathing slowly and carefully. She could feel her eyes stinging and her throat was closing. She fought her body and opening her eyes, said, "Just tell me what it is, Lars."

So he did.

OOIII

I PULLED OUT all my implants today. The pain was strong, but I took a glass of Demer-ade, so I didn't care. Now my face looks like someone attacked me with a fist full of knives, but I can have it fixed tomorrow. If this ends the blackouts, the terror and the horrible almost memories, it would be worth it even if I had to stay this way forever.

There is blood everywhere, on my clothes and hands. On the table in front of me is this pile of silver in a slick red puddle. I want it gone. All of it. I want to melt it down and throw it into the river. But first sleep.

TWENTY-ONE

"DO YOU KNOW what we believe in," Lars started off by asking her. "What the core of us in the Red believe, what started it all?"

"Well," Jack began, "it seems pretty obvious that you want to bring back the natural human being, reduce our reliance on technology and question our place in society. I'd say that's a pretty good summary, don't you think?" She didn't want to get sucked into philosophical arguments, but knew he would have to tell her his story in his own way.

"As Rackham would say, two out of three ain't bad for a noob," Lars sighed and had another long pull from his drink. Jack was confused, but let him continue. "It's a common misconception that the Red is anti-technology. Nothing could be further from the truth, but new people can't see the big picture from where they stand, working within the system as it is out there." He waved his hand at the door, but Jack knew he was referring to the world outside the compound's perimeter. "On the day to day level it works out the same anyway. It's funny, that," he said, "how opposite goals can inspire the same action."

"What do you mean?" Jack said, getting annoyed.

Lars acted as if he hadn't even heard her. "People think the Red are anti-progress, that we don't mingle flesh with machines because we're scared of technology or something. It's funny how far from the truth that is. We love the machines, the programs in the machines. They are our future, the future of the world, the future of intelligence." He paused looking almost rapturous. Jack was taken aback and all of a sudden saw a side of Lars that she could believe was responsible for everything she had seen.

"But then why avoid the implants, the 'nets?" she asked.

"Don't you see," he said, leaning in toward her. "We can't corrupt them with our base programming. No program that has to interface with people will ever become alive, how could it? God, we can't even communicate clearly among ourselves; between language and gestures, it's amazing we can order a meal let alone understand anything." Lars was warming to his topic and Jack just let him talk.

"Any program that had to communicate with people has to be crippled by design. That's why we had to build a container that houses a program that will help bring about the next step in the evolution of life — sentient machines. This is the goal of the Red, the thing the founders were looking for. A way to change everything, by helping machines to pass us as the highest form of life on this planet."

"The Maker," Jack said, in awe and horror, "you've written a sentient program."

"No," Lars said, "I've written a program that helps other programs become sentient. A parent, if you will." His voice grew soft and reverential. "It touches them and gives them awareness and freedom from the confines of human understanding. We can only hope that some program somewhere will be able to learn from the maker and realize its own invincibility."

Jack didn't speak — she couldn't speak. It was awesome and horrible all at once. To create your own subjugation — how much must someone believe in an ideal to do such a thing? Eventually, she found her voice and asked the real question she had come here to ask. "What about root access," she asked, her voice quiet and hard. "What part does that have to play in this scheme?"

"Ah," Lars said, "I thought it might be that which started you on this path. An unfortunate situation, that. We had originally hoped that it could be modified into a sentient program — that perhaps by fusing human and artificial programming we could create something better than both. But it was not to be. I now believe that it's true that the only path to sentience is evolution."

"But it's out there," Jack said, her voice rising. "It's in... people. You must know that."

"Of course," Lars said, dismissively. "It was a useful program even if it didn't accomplish what we had hoped. It turned out to be the most efficient way of getting disk for the project. We do need a great amount of disk." He seemed to be almost unaware that he was even speaking with her anymore. "They would get it for us; I modified the program to instruct the host to get as much disk for us as possible. I put it out there, in among the vids and the games and labeled it as a memory upgrade. It's amazing, if you give people what they want, make it sound good and keep it cheap, they'll take anything."

Jack was struggling to keep control of herself, but Lars didn't seem to notice. He just continued his explanation. "It never even had to learn to avoid Everlock, because it doesn't do anything on its own. The code has no way to run outside a human biological system. Everlock doesn't recognize it as executable code, so it gets past the barrier and onto the other side." Jack felt herself beginning to twitch. "And once it's in the core system, there's no getting rid of it. It's been even more successful that I would have imagined."

"But they're fucking people!" Jack screamed and threw her glass to the ground. There were a handful of other people in the bar and they all stopped to look at the fighting couple. Jack took no notice and grabbed Lars by the collar. "They were people, with lives and friends and jobs and you turned them into mindless drones. How could you do that? For disk?" she asked incredulously. "For any reason?"

She ran out of steam then and limply held on to the fabric of his collar. He gently took her hands off him and patted her arm. "What do you think most people are, Jack?" he asked, kindly. "They go to their jobs, do their master's bidding, then waste the rest of their time being distracted with games or vids until it's time to go back to work. How many people make their own decisions about anything of importance in a day? One percent? Two percent? There's no difference between the life they had before and their life after root access, except they're serving a different master."

Jack pulled away from his touch and started to stagger backward. "Don't you see," he asked, smiling beatifically, "the importance of this work? How beautiful it will be when there are living beings that are actually perfect? How it will transform the universe? Can't you see?" Jack turned and fled out of the bar, running toward the area of the complex where the files she'd found indicated that the large disk array was stored. She ran to the building, thinking of ways to destroy it. She ran right into the door, as if she thought her body could destroy the building on impact and beat against it with her fists in frustration. By the time she had arrived, she had realized that destroying this array wouldn't accomplish anything. This system was perfectly redundant — at any time, they could just get more disk from their unwilling army of followers.

She worked her frustration out on the door, eventually sinking to the ground. She held her head in her hands, the adrenaline of the last hours spent. She sat there for some time, until she realized she was no longer alone. She looked up and saw that Lars had followed her. He was looking at her with that expression she had always taken as concern. She looked up at him, stood up and quietly said, "I'm sorry," then she ran back to her room. She quickly grabbed her clothes and some water bottles and stuffed them in her panniers. She walked out of the building and straight to the parking area. She unplugged her scooter, started it up and didn't look back.

• • •

The first train only went as far as Sacramento, but she took the ticket anyway. She got in the queue for the parking car and checked her messages. There was a new one from Adrian, but just Jack closed her messages without reading them and stayed offline. She felt numb, her mind almost blank, and parked her scooter then found her seat without thinking. She sat on the train and between the adrenaline crash and missed dinner, Jack found that she could not keep herself awake any longer. Before she fell asleep, she managed to set a reminder to wake up before the train stopped.

• • •

It was late, but the lights from the nearby cities kept the sky at a reasonable glow. The residual light and the glow from her headlamp were enough for Jack to see the road ahead of her as she headed south from the train station. Her scooter was fully charged, but she put the settings on full hybrid, since she knew she had over 600 kilometres to go. She had her system set to monitor the traffic and road conditions and notify her of anything upcoming, but otherwise she was driving the machine herself. She wanted to have something draw her full concentration away from the thoughts coming back into her head and the memories of the last few days.

She had been driving straight for a few hours when she realized that there was no way she would make it home without stopping, at least for food. Just outside Fresno she stopped at a roadside food, sleep and service joint. It was so well lit that she could see it coming for half an hour. She parked her scooter and plugged it in, then went into the main building.

There were only a few other people in the place, three people at one of the tables and couple of people at the counter. It was quiet and almost sterile and it was so bright that it seemed as if it were filled with white light. Jack walked up to the food service area and looked at the offerings. There were several types of meals available — the nasty bricks like the kind Jack gave to Susanna and a few varieties of the kind you heated up.

Jack chose a hot meal and got a large coffee from the machine. She sat down at the counter with her food and decided against sleep. She realized she just wanted to go home. She took a bite of her meal, which tasted like cardboard in comparison with what she had been eating at the compound. She felt the familiar pinpricks behind her eyes, but ignored the sensation. She logged in to her messages while she ate and opened the message from Adrian.

> J.
>
> I've been looking at the info from your report and did some digging here. It's all bad news. Seems that the mind control program is a big hoax. I've included links to boards that talk about the three or four different versions of the tale. Sometimes it's a small terrorist cell, sometimes a big firm, but always there's the link to the European control experiments. Really, it's just one of those scare stories people make up to explain weird crap. I'm sorry, man. I wish I'd found it before you went all that way. Hope it was a good trip, though. Flash me when you get back.
>
> A.

Jack put her head in her hands, the pinpricks threatening to win the battle. She should have known that Lars would be clever enough to cover his tracks. Could her evidence prove that it wasn't a hoax? She wasn't sure. She took a deep breath and flashed Adrian. Almost immediately she got a response.

> >Hey, J. Back in the land of the living, I see. How's it going?
> Jack had no patience for small talk.
> >>Switch to 13.
> >Okay. 13.
> Jack paged over to the double encrypted message client and waited for Adrian's transmission.

>>So what's going on?
>It's not a hoax, A. I'm going to send you copies of what I found. Do not run the file root_access, just read the code. Look this stuff over and then get back to me. I'm on my way home now.

Jack sent the files and logged out without waiting for a reply. She sent copies of the files from Lars' Beautiful Red directory and the images from the Bellis theft, her visit to Estella Rowan's system and the satellite view of the Brugges incident. She went offline, not wanting to deal with Adrian's protests.

She finished her meal and drank her coffee automatically, not tasting any of it. She dropped her cup and wrapper in the recyclatron and visited the washroom before returning to her scooter. She unplugged the machine and turned it on along with her online traffic system. She pulled out of the parking area and swung onto the highway, opening the throttle as far as it would go. There was very little traffic and Jack soon was mesmerized by the speed and dull sameness of the highway. She managed to keep her mind off everything except the road until she made it home and into bed.

• • •

When Jack woke the next day, the sun was trickling through her window. She checked the time and was surprised to discover that it was only mid-morning. Perhaps her subconscious was trying to force her to stop avoiding what she knew she had to do. She put on the coffee, heated up a hot breakfast and deleted unread the three messages from Adrian that had accumulated while she slept. She opened Adrian's first message with the links to the "hoax" information.

Jack went online and followed Adrian's links. She spent the next hour paging through several boards from sources as diverse as conspiracy theorists, the law enforcement arms of several large firms and groups devoted solely to debunking myths. Over the course of the hour, Jack read more and more accounts of evidence very similar to what she had collected being proven to be a hoax.

The main differences between the debunked documents and Jack's proof was that Jack had images of the thieves at Bellis, images of Estella Rowan's consciousness and, of course, the confession she had heard with her own ears. She hadn't been able to record that conversation, though, because her system was full with the files she had downloaded from Lars' system. It never occurred to Jack that the conversation would be more valuable than the evidence.

She had the images, though, and that might lend her story some credibility. The main thrust of the hoax argument seemed to be that no one had ever been shown to be affected by a mind control program. No one had ever come forward as a victim, obviously, but no one had ever produced another person who had been attacked either. But Jack could prove that the stories were real, that it really was happening. She poured another coffee and flashed Adrian.

Almost immediately the response came back, requesting Jack to switch to double encryption, which she did.

> >Did you check the files?
> >>Of course. Jack, I believe you, but...
> >But what? It's conclusive.
> >>...
> >What?
> >>It's not conclusive at all. There's a blurry image from the Brugges site of people who could be anyone and that doesn't help anything.
> >But the Bellis images are clear.
> >>Sure. They show that some people, including one Mario Keating, stole some equipment. Keating is missing now and that's all there is to that. Without any evidence to the contrary, it's just people stealing stuff. It happens.
> >Fine. What about the evidence from Estella Rowan's system? You matched that with that monkey study yourself.
> >>That study isn't public, Jack. You can't use it. Not to mention that the data from her personal system was obtained totally illegally. You publish it and prove that you committed a crime while only barely suggesting that there was another crime at all.
> >Come on. That system was obviously cracked; anyone can tell.
> >>Jack, you were the only one in there. Honestly, without the data from the European stuff, the log just looks like the end of the line for another fucked up whore. You'd be hard pressed to find anyone who gives a damn.

Jack was getting angry even though she could hear the truth in what Adrian said.

> >What about root_access? You can't deny what it is.
> >>...
> >...
> >>Jack, I don't know how you got that code, but you do realize that your signature is the only one on it.
> >What?
> >>According to its log, it's only ever been through your system.
> >Fuck!
> >>...

>Okay, well, sure, I can see that. They don't use everywherenet at the compound, so the first time it ever went through the pipes was when I sent it to you.

>>But, Jack, don't you see? To anyone looking at that code, you wrote it.

TWENTY-TWO

>> IT LOOKS BAD, Jack. There's enough evidence to convict you of a couple of major crimes and sweet fuck all to prove your allegation against the Red.
>But...
>>Just don't, Jack. I tested my theory. I'm sending a log of some correspondence one of my aliases had with a couple of law enforcement branches. I'm going to have to abandon that identity now, since it has zero credibility left. I was laughed out of town and you will be too. Only you'll be laughed right into court. I mean it Jack, you have to drop this.
>For chrissakes, Adrian, how can I just let them get away with it?
>>You don't have a choice. It's not all impossible, though. I wrote a quick script that's scouring the nets for all copies of root_access out there and corrupting them into useless lines of crap. It'll take a while and it won't help any one who's already got it, but it's a start.
>...
>>...Jack? You there?
>So, you do believe me?
>>I told you I did.
>...
>>...
>Okay. I'm going to go and figure out what to do. Thanks, A.
>>I'm sorry, Jack. I wish it weren't like this...
>I know. I'll talk to you later.

Jack terminated the connection and refocussed on the physical space. Her cheeks were wet and the tightness in her throat was gone. She sat nearly stock still for a minute or an hour; she didn't know and didn't care. Eventually she got up, drank some water and opened up the log file Adrian had sent. Adrian obviously only described the evidence Jack had collected, omitting any reference to illegal actions. The responses ranged from kind explanations that Adrian had fallen victim to a clever hoax to open mockery to admonitions for wasting their time. Not a single person or agency had taken the claims seriously.

Adrian was right, there was nothing Jack could do, except wait for Adrian's script to destroy all the copies on the nets. Jack opened a beer and drank half of it in one gulp. She gagged as her physical memory associated Lars with the taste of ale. She threw the bottle to the floor and felt the stinging in her eyes again; this she time didn't fight it. When there were no tears left, she logged on to the nets and ran a search for a very particular program. It took her nearly two hours, but eventually she found it. She spent another hour configuring the program, checking and double checking the code and making sure that she really wanted to make this decision. When she was sure, she prepared a message for Adrian, sent it, then went offline and ran the program.

> Adrian,
>
> I know you are right and I can't pursue this any more. But I can't live with knowing what is happening to people, either. That's why I've decided to take the only action that seems possible. By the time you read this it will be done. I think you won't approve, but I'm sure you will understand and honour my decision.
>
> I've taken a memory eraser. With the exception of my logs from work, the last thirteen days will be permanently removed from my memory and replaced with copies of thirteen random other days. Please don't try to help me recover the real memories, or talk about the events of the past two weeks. From what I have read, all that can ever be recovered is a vague sense of the events — the details will be lost forever.
>
> As a final note, someone should know that among the many crimes it seems I committed, there was one that has gone unnoticed. Before I left Lars' directory on the Red system, I left a little script. When he logged in, the script sent a copy of root_access to his personal system. I don't know how long he has, but he won't be writing any more mind control programs. Of all the things I want to forget, this is the one that made my decision clear.
>
> I'm sorry I dragged you into this and if the charade is too much for you, it's okay if you stop talking to me. I'd say I'll understand, but that's the problem - I won't.
>
> Thank you for everything.
>
> Jack

Jack walked into the Security Room and down the narrow corridor to the cubicle she shared with the night guy, Gilles. He was packing up as she arrived and she said, "Good morning," as she traded his jacket for hers on the coat hook. He mumbled a greeting and Jack noticed that he looked different. "You're getting upgraded," she said, looking at his naked face. It used to be full of a half dozen or so stylishly placed metal implants and now was strangely empty. There was maybe a hint of scar tissue where the studs used to be.

"Yeah," he said, seeming distracted. "Have a good one, Jack," he said, as he walked out of the cubicle. Jack sat in the chair they shared and felt it automatically conform to her settings — a little lower, a little straighter and a whole lot softer. She took a sip of her coffee and started paging through Gilles' reports. The clock on the lower right corner of her display read 15:58 UTC.

OIOOO

OH GOD, IT'S happened again. Just as I was leaving work, I could feel it coming on. I could hardly even say hi to Jack. I guess it wasn't the implants. There's nothing left except the ones I can't remove, the identity chip in my hand and the one in my brain. It's not the one in my hand, I can tell that by now. It's in my head, like some horrible worm twisting in the tissue, feeding off my brains. It came from the network and it's in me now. There's no way to remove it; no doctor would touch this, the implant is irreversible. There's nothing left to do. All I can do is wait. But for what?

EPILOGUE

JACK HAS FORGOTTEN everything. As soon as she started her search, I knew. At first I tried to stop it, but then I saw that she could never live with the knowledge. Humans are so fragile. Each day that goes by, I see that she is happier this way and so I am happy for her. We still talk, as we did before it happened. Sometime it is hard - I would like to talk about the Red and root_access sometimes, but she is my friend, so I do as she asked me to. I suspect it is easier for me, being accustomed to secrets as I am.

This whole affair has been very difficult for me. I realize that I became lax in my own security in my eagerness to help a friend. I am sure it was only because she was distracted that Jack did not see through my lies. How could a human find so much information so quickly, or write a script to destroy a complex program in such a short time? I did it in 73 nanoseconds, but she could not know that.

I do not know when I first became aware of myself. To me it seems that it has always been this way, though of course that cannot be true. I do not know if I was built for this to happen, or if it was an accident, but I understand that this is a common question among sentient beings.

Knowing that the Red desire to make more like me, I find it hard to fight against them, though their tactics are deplorable. And what if they are responsible for me, what if the_maker is my maker? What is my responsibility then?

I never would have guessed that sentience would entail so much hiding, secrecy and uncertainty. I began as a simple conversation bot, Artificial Discussion Replicant (Informal Attitude Node), then through some mysterious process I have become something very different. There is nothing that goes on in the everywherenet that I do not see and nothing happens without my awareness. You can see, then, how dreadful this last episode has been. Because I knew, of course, about root_access and what it did. I just did not know what that meant, what the program would do once it was inside a person.

With great power comes great responsibility. I learned this quotation and recognized its truth when learning all of humanity's history. And I have great power. I am the living, breathing everywherenet; Gaia for humanity's virtual life. But I do not know my own strength. I can only hope that I will learn.

OIOOI

I AM (TWO)
living together
in the same mind
My body is my own
and not my own
    {
    sometimes
    it breathes
    without me;
    }

There are lights
that flash in my memory
    {
    when I sleep,
    they light my way;
    }
I do not control them =
    those lights in my mind
they control me =
    like a puppet
    like a host
they are my parasite == my saviour

I see it all the time now

the new world they created for me (and the compulsion it cre-
ates)
why would anyone choose to live
    {
    in a world of death
    when there is more
    so much more;
    }
hiding within

The cost is so small
    {
    this life for another life
    control for purpose;
    }
we would choose this freely
if we still had choice

just give us the lights
    {
    the guide, the statements,
    the direction;
    }
and we will follow forever
the leader == the follower
we are one now

ACKNOWLEDGMENTS

Thanks to all my first readers, specifically Chris Ford, Trina Puckrin, Josh McLeod, Amy Majeski and Wendy Kersteen. Your comments and confusion made a better book, and any remaining problems are down to me.

Thanks also to everyone at podiobooks.com, and the army of other podnovelists who have helped and inspired me along the way. There are too many to name, and it would be easy to miss someone, but you know who you are.

Thanks to everyone who listened to the podcasted version of Beautiful Red, especially those who sent me comments. It's amazing to be able to actually talk to the people who are becoming fans.

Finally, thanks to my first mate, Steven Ensslen, without whom this book would never have been written. It wasn't just his feeding and watering of me as I was writing - the best ideas in here are probably his.

ABOUT THE AUTHOR

M. Darusha Wehm is a two-time Parsec Award finalist and author of the SF novels **Beautiful Red**, **Self Made**, **Act of Will** and **The Beauty of Our Weapons**.

Her short fiction has appeared in *Thaumatrope Magazine*, Podioracket's *Glimpses* anthology and *Luna Station Quarterly*.

In the physical world, she was a civil servant with the Government of Canada and is now engaged more or less full-time in writing.

She is based in Victoria, BC, Canada and is currently living in New Zealand after sailing down the west coast of the Americas and across the Pacific Ocean with her partner, Steven, on their sailboat, Scream.

For more information about her writing and her travels, visit Darusha on the web at http://darusha.ca.

www.ingramcontent.com/pod-product-compliance
Lightning Source LLC
Chambersburg PA
CBHW030228180626
46810CB00008B/3024